ON AIR WITH Zoe Washington

ON AIR WITH Zoe Washington

JANAE MARKS

KATHERINE TEGEN BOOKS
An Imprint of HarperCollins Publishers

Katherine Tegen Books is an imprint of HarperCollins Publishers.

Library of Congress Cataloging-in-Publication Data
Names: Marks, Janae, author. | Marks, Janae
  From the Desk of Zoe Washington.
Title: On air with Zoe Washington / Janae Marks.
Description: First edition. | New York : Katherine Tegen
  Books, [2023] | Audience: Ages 8–12. | Audience: Grades
  4–6. | Summary: Follows fourteen-year-old Zoe and
  her recently exonerated father as they build their new
  relationship and work to open a restaurant together.
Identifiers: LCCN 2022029562 | ISBN 9780063212312 (hardcover)
Subjects: CYAC: Fathers and daughters—Fiction. |
  Podcasts—Fiction. | Restaurants—Fiction. | Family
  life—Fiction. | African Americans—Fiction.
Classification: LCC PZ7.1.M3722 On 2023 | DDC [Fic]—dc23
LC record available at https://lccn.loc.gov/2022029562

Typography by Laura Mock
22 23 24 25 26 LBC 5 4 3 2 1

First Edition

To all of my amazing readers
who asked for more of Zoe's story:
This is for you.

**Excerpt from Boston Public Radio's
Interview Hour with John Gallagher**
Aired on June 20

John Gallagher: Welcome back to Boston Public
Radio's Interview Hour. We're here with Marcus
Johnson and his fourteen-year-old daughter, Zoe.
Before the break, we talked to Marcus about how he
was wrongfully convicted of murder fifteen years ago,
and recently exonerated. Now I'd like to ask Zoe a
few questions since she actually played an important
role in Marcus's release. Zoe, what made you want to
investigate your father's crime in the first place? You
were only, what, twelve years old at the time?

Zoe: Yup. Well, once I realized Marcus might be
innocent of the crime, I had to know the truth. I'd
never investigated anything before, but I don't
know—I was just determined.

Marcus Johnson: Zoe's *very* determined. I didn't
want her looking into my case, but she did it anyway.

John: [laughter] It's a good quality to have. Still, what you did is impressive for a kid.

Zoe: I guess, but I had some help from my grandma and best friend Trevor. What kept me going was how much I hated the idea of Marcus being in prison if he hadn't done anything wrong. Sometimes I think about what my life would been like if he'd never been arrested for a crime he didn't commit. Like, what if he'd been able to be my dad my whole life? But at least now we get to have time together.

John: When you first found out that Marcus was being exonerated, how did you feel?

Zoe: When the judge read the verdict, I was in the courtroom, sitting in the row right behind Marcus. My parents were next to me. I think I screamed and then started crying when the judge said, "not guilty." It's kind of a blur now, but I was so excited.

John: I bet.

Zoe: It was like everything I did two years ago, and all the waiting since then had finally paid off.

John: Now that Marcus is out of prison, what do you look forward to the most?

Zoe: So many things. Spending more time together in person. Listening to music. Cooking and baking. Actually, we both are working at Ari's Cakes in Beacon Hill this summer, so . . . if you're listening, you should come by!

John: Zoe brought some of her treats to the studio, so I can attest to how delicious her baking is. I will definitely make a trip out to Ari's Cakes. Well, thank you, Marcus and Zoe. We wish you both the best. [Music starts] We'll be right back after after these messages.

Chapter One

If someone had told ten-year-old me that in four years I'd have a bakery job and that my birth dad—who I didn't even know at the time—would be my coworker, I would've looked at them like they had two heads. It was totally unbelievable. But now, it was happening.

"Hey, Little T!" Marcus said as he got out of the passenger side of Grandma's car.

"Hey, Big T!" I gave him a hug.

"Little T" and "Big T" were our new nicknames for each other—short versions of Little Tomato, what Marcus called me when he wrote me letters from prison, and Big Tomato.

We got into the car, and I said hello to Grandma. She had agreed to drive me and Marcus to Ari's Cakes, since Marcus had gotten his driver's license reactivated a week ago but didn't have a car to drive yet.

"Ready to go?" Grandma asked from the driver's seat. Her earrings, which were made of small translucent shells, jangled as she twisted in her seat to talk to me.

"Yup!"

"Are you excited?" I asked Marcus from the back seat. "Or nervous?"

"I guess both," he said with a laugh. "But more excited. It'll be nice to make cupcakes in the kitchen instead of the boring, tasteless meals I helped cook in prison."

"Is that the only thing you're excited about?" I asked. "The baking?"

Marcus pretended to think. "Yeah." He paused. "I think that's it."

I leaned forward in my seat and nudged him in the shoulder.

He laughed. "Of course I'm excited to work with you." He looked back at me and smiled. "It's the best part of this whole job."

I smiled back. "Same here."

When we got to Beacon Hill, Marcus and I said goodbye to Grandma and walked inside the bakery. I breathed in the comforting smells of sugar and frosting, mixed with coffee. I looked around the shop and soaked it all in. The cupcakes displayed behind the glass counter in a rainbow of colors, including my Froot Loop cupcake recipe, which Ari still sold two years later. The pale-blue walls that matched the Ari's Cakes T-shirt I was wearing. The little bud vases holding fresh flowers that sat on every table and next to the cash register. The ambient, cheery music playing lightly over the speakers. This was my home away from home.

I waved at Gabe, who was currently taking orders. There were a few customers in line already.

"Zoe! Perfect timing," he said.

"Hey," I said. "I'm just gonna put my backpack away."

I followed Marcus to the kitchen and left my bag in a cubby.

Ariana waved at us from across the kitchen, where she was helping Vincent with something. "Hey, you two. Marcus, grab an apron and come over. We have a big order to work on. Zoe, Gabe will get you settled up front."

"Okay." I stood there for a second and watched Marcus put his apron on over his jeans and black T-shirt. I wished I got to wear one, but since I wasn't working in the kitchen, it wasn't part of my uniform anymore.

I was finally old enough to work full-time at the bakery all summer and get paychecks just like every other employee. But because I wasn't sixteen years old, I wasn't legally allowed to bake in the kitchen. I'd gotten away with helping in the kitchen as an intern because I hadn't been an official employee. I'd only helped for a couple of hours, once a week. Now that I was old enough, I had to follow the rules. I'd work Monday through Friday at the front of the shop. At least I'd get to do more than fold boxes and refill napkin dispensers. I was allowed to take cupcake orders, pack them, *and* use the cash register.

"All right, Little T," Marcus said. "Wish me luck."

"You don't need luck. You got this."

Marcus grinned wide. "You too."

As I stood there watching Marcus go over to Ariana and Vincent, I felt like the parent watching their kid go off to their first day of school. There was a tiny bit of envy in my gut since Marcus would get to bake. I wondered what the big order Ariana mentioned was, and if it involved a special recipe or interesting decorations. It suddenly hit me how much I wanted to bake, instead of handing out the cupcakes up front. But there was nothing I could do about that. In two years, I'd be allowed to work in the kitchen again. And in the meantime, I'd bake as much as I could at home.

Back up front, I dove right into work. The line of customers kept growing with the morning rush, so I helped pour coffee and box up cupcakes while Gabe worked the register. Once things quieted down, he showed me how the register worked. It was simple once I figured out which buttons to press.

"How's it going out here?" Ariana asked me a while later.

"Great!" I said.

"Awesome. If you want to take a lunch break now, you can. I told Marcus the same."

"Okay."

Just then, Marcus came out of the kitchen without his apron. "Want to grab a slice of pizza or something?" he asked me.

"Yes, please."

When we got outside, I pulled out my phone.

"Who are you calling?" Marcus asked.

"Oh, I'm going to search for a pizza place. There's an app that tells you about the best restaurants in the area you're in."

Marcus laughed. "Right. There're apps for everything." He pulled his new cell phone out of his pocket. "Before I was in prison, I had this flip phone that still had actual buttons. Now I can unlock this phone with my face. It's amazing."

"There's a pizza place with good ratings a two-minute walk away," I said.

"Sounds great."

We walked a few blocks, past restaurants, a small grocery store, a flower shop, and lots of brownstones.

When we got to the pizza place, we each ordered two pepperoni slices and a soda. I asked for pineapple to be added to my pizza. Then we found a nearby bench to sit on. It was such a perfect day out. Sunny, not too hot, and slightly breezy. I loved Boston in the summer.

"Did you know they have a Black Heritage Trail around here?" Marcus asked after we spent a few minutes quietly eating our pizza.

"What's that?" I asked.

"It's a tour you can take of different African American landmarks around here. There used to be a community of free Black people in Beacon Hill, before the Civil War."

"How do you know that?"

"My parents took me here a few times as a kid," Marcus said. "We did the self-guided tour. They liked to talk to me and my brother about Black history growing up."

"That's cool." I wiped some pizza sauce off my chin

with a napkin. "You should show me the trail. We can do it together during our lunch breaks."

"I like that idea." Marcus smiled. "How's your first day at the bakery going?"

"Pretty good. It was busy up front, which made the time fly. What about you? Do you like working in the kitchen?"

"Yeah. Vincent's showing me the ropes."

There was that envy again. I wished I could help Vincent mix cupcake batter.

"But you know," Marcus continued, "being in a professional kitchen is bringing up this dream that I've had for a while. I can't stop thinking about it."

"What dream?"

"I'd really love to open up my own restaurant someday," he said.

"Oh wow, really?"

"Yeah. Sometimes when I couldn't fall asleep in my cell, I'd close my eyes and make up possible menus. Or I'd think about what the inside of the restaurant could look like."

"What kind of food would you want it to have?" I asked.

"I'm thinking barbecue. It wouldn't even need to be

a big place to start. Growing up, there was this hole-in-the-wall Haitian spot not far from our house. It was tiny inside, only enough space for two tables and the counter where they served the food. Plus, a fridge with beverages. But it was always crowded because the food was so good." Marcus nodded. "Yeah. A small barbecue spot would be perfect."

I smiled. "I love it. You'd *have* to serve the ribs you made at your birthday party."

"Yeah. I think I could do it. Come up with a menu that people would like."

"You could *totally* do it."

And then it hit me: an idea so perfect, it made me drop my pizza slice.

Chapter Two

"*You all right?*" *Marcus asked* as I picked the pizza slice up from my lap. Luckily it had fallen there and not on the ground. Though I was pretty sure I saw disappointment in a nearby pigeon's eye.

I put the slice back into the pizza box and took a couple of napkins from Marcus's hand.

"What if . . ." I started as I quickly wiped tomato sauce off my jeans. "What if we opened a restaurant *together*? I could be in charge of the desserts." Maybe if it was our own restaurant, I could get back into the kitchen. It would be amazing to be the pastry chef of my very own place.

"I could definitely come up with a dessert menu. In a barbecue restaurant, we could do . . ." I paused to think. ". . . a multilayered red velvet cake, creamy banana pudding, peach cobbler. We could even do different homemade ice creams. What do you think?" I looked up at Marcus with pleading eyes, willing him to say yes.

"Zoe," Marcus said, his face suddenly serious.

My insides flip-flopped. *He hates this idea,* I thought. *He probably thinks I'm too young for this. I need to convince him that he's wrong!*

But then he said, "Opening a restaurant with you would be my biggest dream come true."

My heart leaped. "Seriously?"

"Seriously. There's nobody else I'd want to oversee the desserts."

I grinned at him and then picked up my pizza so I could finish eating it.

"There's one other thing I really want to do, if I'm able to open a restaurant," Marcus said.

"What?"

"I want to hire people who were previously incarcerated to work there. As many as I can."

"What do you mean? Other exonerees?" I asked, meaning other people like Marcus who'd been charged with crimes they didn't actually commit.

"Sure, exonerees. But I'd also like to hire people who weren't innocent of their crimes but served their time and are ready to do better."

"Why?" I didn't say the rest of my question out loud. *Why would you want criminals working in our restaurant?*

"I mentioned this in my letters, but I made some friends in prison," Marcus said. "Most of them were guilty of their crimes. But they weren't bad people. They'd made mistakes. Big, life-changing mistakes."

I nodded.

"Some of them had really tough childhoods. Not that it's an excuse, but for a lot of people, the circumstances of their upbringing led them to whatever mistake they made.

"Take my friend Shawn," Marcus continued. "He spent his entire childhood in and out of different foster homes. Most of his foster parents were only in it for the money. He wasn't always treated well. Sometimes he was treated badly. When he got older, he joined a local gang. They made him feel like he was part of a family, you know? I think if he'd had a real family all along, he wouldn't have felt the need to join the gang. But he did, and they committed crimes. Shawn was part of that, and one night, even though he wasn't the one with the weapon, he was arrested. Now, though? He's a changed man. We had some deep conversations. He wishes he hadn't felt like the gang was all he had, that it was the only option, when it wasn't. He takes full responsibility for his past actions, but now he wants to help foster care youth like him when he gets released. He wants to try to prevent the same thing from happening again."

"Wow," I said.

"There are a lot of people like that, who are waiting for the chance to build a better life," Marcus said. "It's tough, though, because people on the outside judge. They think, 'once a criminal, always a criminal.' But if they were more open-minded, they'd see that that's not the case for a lot of folks."

He was talking about me. I was one of those people. But . . . what if Marcus was wrong? How could he know who really wanted to do better?

"And then there's the issue with previously incarcerated people having trouble finding jobs," Marcus continued. "Employers don't want to employ someone with a record. Even exonerees, who should get their records cleaned up, have trouble because they were still in prison for many years and have no recent job experience or training. I got lucky, with my lawyer and Ariana setting me up with my two part-time jobs."

Marcus's other part-time job, which his Innocence Project lawyer had connected him with, was with a legal nonprofit organization. He worked in their office, answering the phone, filing, and doing other stuff like that.

"If I can, I'd really like to pay it forward and help others get back on their feet after they've been in prison."

I thought about everything Marcus had just said. My first instinct was no, I wouldn't want to work alongside someone who had committed a crime. How would I know they wouldn't do it again? How could I trust that they really wanted to do better? And how would I know that I'd be safe around them?

But Marcus was talking about giving people a second chance. A chance to start over and build a better life. If there were people out there who had served their time, who felt bad about what they had done and truly wanted a better life, then why not help them?

It made me think of my best friend Trevor and how I gave him a second chance after he hurt my feelings a couple of summers ago. Now our friendship was stronger than ever. If I hadn't let him make up for his past mistake, who knows where we'd be?

It really wasn't the same, though. I still felt unsure. What should I say to Marcus? I didn't want to squash his dream, especially when he was thinking about helping people.

But then Marcus said, "Hopefully we can open a restaurant in a few years. When you're done with college."

Wait, what?

"College?" I asked. "But that's so long from now! We should try to open a restaurant sooner!"

Marcus frowned. "I don't know if that's possible."

"Why not?"

He shrugged. "To be honest, I spent more time dreaming of menus and not a lot of time figuring out the logistics of opening a restaurant."

"Let's do that now, then. Figure out the logistics. Do you really want to wait . . ." I did the math in my head. ". . . eight more years to do this? After all that you've been through, you deserve this. I mean, this is my dream now too, and I don't want to wait."

I felt like Veruca Salt from the *Willy Wonka & the Chocolate Factory* movie. Now that the idea of co-owning a restaurant was in my head, I wanted it now.

Marcus's expression turned serious. "You still have to

finish school, though, Zoe. No dropping out to help run a restaurant."

"Of course," I said. "Lots of kids have after-school jobs, so this could be mine. And I bet this would make an awesome college essay."

"With all you're accomplishing, Little T, I don't think you'll have any trouble getting into college."

I beamed.

"All right." Marcus exhaled. "It won't hurt to start looking into how you go about opening a restaurant. But we have to ask your parents first. You can't be involved with this unless you have their blessing."

"No problem," I said immediately. "I'll ask them tonight."

Marcus laughed. "You really do go after what you want, don't you?"

"Yup." It had worked when I wanted the truth about Marcus. Why couldn't it work now?

"Let me give your mom a call first," Marcus said. "I want her to hear about this from me."

"Okay."

He glanced at his watch. "We should head back. Our lunch break is about to be over."

We threw away our empty pizza box and soda cans and headed back to Ari's Cakes.

This time, when Marcus went to the kitchen to put his apron back on and start baking again, I wasn't envious at all.

Soon I'd be a pastry chef in our own restaurant. I was sure of it.

Chapter Three

To celebrate my first full day at Ari's Cakes, Mom and Dad took me out to dinner in Davis Square. We went to our favorite taco place and ordered a bunch of things to share—several tacos, fresh guacamole that a cook made right in front of us, Mexican street corn, and a black bean salad.

"Tell us all about your day," Mom said between bites of chips and guacamole.

"It was great," I said. "I learned the cash register super fast. After lunch, Gabe let me do it all on my own."

"That's my girl," Dad said. "Did you like having Marcus there?"

"Yeah. He got to work in the kitchen. We ate lunch together, though."

"Nice."

I suddenly wondered if Dad felt bad that I was spending more time with Marcus now that he was out of prison. It wasn't like Marcus was replacing him or anything. He had to know that. And anyway, he was the one who just asked about Marcus.

I turned to Mom. "Speaking of Marcus, did he call you about anything?"

"No," she said. "Why?"

I was tempted to spill all about the restaurant idea, but Marcus had said he wanted Mom to hear it from him first. Hopefully he'd call sometime tonight. "No reason." I took a bite of a taco.

"Are you sure?" Mom asked.

"I'm sure," I said, reaching for my lemonade. "Just forget about it."

We went back to eating. When we were done with our meal and waiting for the check, Mom took her cell phone out of her purse. That's when I noticed that it was vibrating with a new call.

"Hey, Marcus, what's up?" she asked when she picked it up.

Finally. I leaned in to hear her side of the conversation better.

"You know, hold on," Mom said to Marcus. "It's loud in here. Can I call you back later?"

No! "We can go outside," I said, pushing my chair back so I could stand up. "Dad can finish waiting for the check. Is that okay?" I turned to him.

"Fine with me," he said.

Mom shrugged and told Marcus to hold on for a second. We went outside and stood next to the restaurant's entrance.

"Oh, really . . . uh-huh . . . uh-huh. Wow. That sounds like a big undertaking . . . Right . . . Oh, I know . . . Well, thanks for telling me." She glanced at me. "I'll definitely talk to Zoe about it . . . Okay, sounds good. Have a good night."

"Did he tell you?" I asked as soon as she hung up. "About his restaurant idea?"

"He sure did," Mom said.

Just then, Dad walked out of the restaurant, sucking on one of the mints that came with the check. "Ready to go?"

We started walking to where we had parked the car.

"What do you think?" I asked Mom.

"Think about what?" Dad asked, and Mom filled him in.

"Marcus and I would make a great team, right?" I asked.

"Sure," Mom said. "But opening a restaurant—that is a lot of work. And you're still young. Even Marcus said he knows this might not happen."

"I know that. But it could happen. And when it does . . ." I was trying to be optimistic. "We can handle it."

"You're such a talented baker, Zoe," Mom said. "And I love how passionate you are. But you don't become a pastry chef at a restaurant overnight. It's a full-time job, and bakers usually go to culinary school first."

"True, but this is going to be a really casual restaurant. We'd serve cake, pies, ice cream, that sort of thing. Nothing I haven't baked before."

"I think what your mom's saying is that you shouldn't feel rushed to have a big baking career," Dad said. "You can, and should, take the time you need to keep learning."

We reached our car, and I frowned at them. "You're saying I can't do it?"

Mom looked at Dad, then at me, and sighed. "Look, if this is Marcus's dream, what he really wants to do, I hope it works out. He deserves to have a regular life and whatever career he wants. If this gets to the point where he has a location and a timeline, and it's looking like it's going to happen? Then we can talk about how you can be involved. But don't get your hopes up, Zo. It's hard to open a restaurant. It could take years."

"I know that." I couldn't help but grin. She wasn't saying no.

When we got in the car, I sent Marcus a text: **So excited to open our restaurant!**

Marcus texted back: :-)

I smiled and made a mental note to show him how to use emojis the next time I saw him.

I knew opening a restaurant would be hard, and it could take a long time. But I was still certain that if anyone could do the impossible, it was me and Marcus.

As soon as I got home, I opened my laptop and searched for the phrase "How to open a restaurant." A bunch of articles came up, and I started skimming through them. One of them talked about creating a business plan. Another was about how to pick the best location. Another talked about restaurant pitfalls. There was so much to figure out, and already I felt overwhelmed. I bookmarked a few articles to share with Marcus, and then closed my laptop.

On my desk next to my laptop was a notebook covered with illustrations of cupcakes and donuts. It was my baking notebook, where I wrote down recipes and ideas. I turned to a new page and, at the top, wrote "Big & Little T Restaurant: Dessert Ideas."

I wrote down everything I'd thought of so far.

red velvet cake

peach cobbler

banana pudding

ice creams (what flavors??)

Reading through the list, everything sounded kind of . . . expected. I wanted to add something that would stand out, like my Froot Loop cupcakes did at Ari's Cakes. Like a signature dessert, something that would make people want to return to our restaurant again and again.

I thought about that scene in the movie *Ratatouille*, when Remy the rat came out into the dining room after the food critic wanted to meet the chef. Of course, he was surprised to see that a rat had cooked for him. That could be me, except the food critic will be surprised that a teenage baker baked the desserts. I could become famous, like Ruby Willow after she won the *Kids Bake Challenge!* show.

I knew I could come up with something amazing. I could spend the rest of the summer experimenting with different flavors and recipes. Then I wouldn't have to feel so bad about not baking at work.

Satisfied with this idea, I closed my notebook. But then I thought of all the articles I had bookmarked for Marcus. I couldn't ignore them and only focus on dessert ideas. We needed to figure out the logistics somehow. We needed help.

And then I realized I knew just the right person to ask for advice.

Chapter Four

Ariana! She was the perfect person to talk to about opening a restaurant, since she had probably gone through a similar process to open her bakery. As soon as I got to work in the morning, I'd ask for her advice.

While I waited outside for Grandma to come pick me up the next day, I heard the familiar sounds of a storm door opening and closing. Trevor's family *still* hadn't fixed that door, but I kind of loved that. It meant I always knew when someone was coming.

I turned around to see who it was. It was my best friend Trevor, and he was wearing a Medford Basketball Camp T-shirt.

"Hey. I didn't get to see you yesterday before you left for work," Trevor said. "How was it?"

"So far, so good," I said. "What about you? How's basketball camp going?" Normally Trevor didn't have a summer activity either. His parents, like mine, usually left him to create his own entertainment. But for this summer, he'd convinced them to let him sign up for the local basketball camp, since he wanted to try out for the high school team in the fall. It wasn't expensive, so they'd agreed to it.

"It's great." He sat on the porch steps next to me. "We do a lot of drills and we're going to play multiple games a week. I know, like, half the kids from our middle school team. And the other half is from Andrews Middle School. It's cool to be able to get to know them now since we'll all be in high school together."

"Awesome. I'm happy for you. But it's also kind of sad that we won't get to hang out all the time this summer, like usual." Sometimes it was annoying to have to figure out how to fill our time. We could only ride our bikes so much. But I was going to miss that. What if the previous summer had been our last chance to spend all our time together, and we hadn't even realized it? We would probably have camp or jobs or other stuff every summer in high school, too.

He shrugged. "I know. But we'll still see each other. And listen, if you ever need someone to taste-test anything, you know I'm always here. *Anytime.*" He rubbed his belly and I laughed.

At least he'd still live right next door.

"Actually," Trevor continued, "I was talking to Maya, and we were saying we should all do a movie night or something. Maybe this Friday?"

"Oh, sure. That sounds fun."

But then I thought, *Wait a minute. He was talking to Maya? Alone?*

I hadn't realized Trevor talked to Maya outside of our group text. Maya was my other best friend. It used to be me, Maya, and Jasmine in a group chat, but Jasmine moved away a couple of summers ago. Since then, Maya and I had been hanging out together with Trevor more. I still spent more time with Trevor because we were neighbors. Plus, Maya was usually gone during the summer—at camp or on vacation with her family. But this summer, her dad was getting a kidney transplant, so Maya had decided to stay home to be here for his recovery.

Why hadn't I known that Trevor and Maya talked separately? Why would they leave me out? It's not like they couldn't be friends without me, but it felt wrong for some reason. Or, not *wrong*, but . . . strange. It was probably nothing, though, so I pushed that feeling aside.

"Okay, cool," Trevor said. "We can do it at my place."

"Great. I'll bring some snacks."

Trevor grinned. "Something with chocolate, okay?"

"Of course."

Just then, Grandma pulled up in her car and waved at us from behind the wheel.

"Gotta go," I told Trevor. "I'll talk to you later."

"Later," Trevor said, and went back inside his house.

Marcus wasn't in the car with Grandma this time since he had his other job on Tuesdays.

While Grandma drove, I told her all about my restaurant plan with Marcus. I also told her what my mom had said.

"You know, baby," Grandma said, "I didn't think you'd be able to find Marcus's alibi witness, and you did that. You can absolutely do anything you put your mind to. I can't wait to see you with that chef's hat on."

I'd known Grandma wouldn't doubt me, but I still smiled extra wide.

"Marcus is a great cook, too," Grandma said. "He's insisted on making me dinner a few times a week, since he's staying in my guest room. I told him he doesn't owe me anything, but the food is excellent, so I can't complain. He's got something special."

We've both got something special, I thought. Together I knew we were unstoppable.

At work, I waited for a chance to talk to Ariana. She was busy running around the bakery throughout the first half of the day, and I got busy working behind the counter with Gabe. I hoped I could catch her during my lunch break, but she was on the phone in her office when it started. Instead of going outside, I decided to sit on a folding chair in the corner of the kitchen while I ate the sandwich, apple, and chips that I'd brought from home.

"We miss you back here, Zoe," Liz said from her work-station. She was one of the regular bakers in the kitchen.

"I miss it too," I said. But it was nice to sit back there and watch everyone work. I watched as Vincent, wearing a black-and-white bandanna today, turned on the huge stand mixer and poured flour inside. Then I watched Liz as she molded flowers out of gum paste. By the time she finished one, it looked so delicate and realistic. I took mental notes so I could try it myself at home sometime.

If I couldn't bake in the Ari's Cakes kitchen, I could still learn by watching everyone else. Eating my lunch inside on the days Marcus wasn't there would be like having my own backstage pass to a professional kitchen. I could even bring my notebook and take notes.

As soon as I saw Ariana leave her office, I jumped up and went over to her.

"Hey, Ariana, do you have a minute?"

"Sure," she said. "What's up?"

I knew I didn't have much time, so I jumped right in. "I was wondering if you could share any advice about opening a restaurant. I know a bakery isn't the same thing, but what did you have to do to get started?"

Ariana narrowed her eyes at me. "Already looking to become my competition?"

"No!" I said. "Not at all!"

Ariana laughed. "I'm just kidding. Trust me, if you open your own bakery one day, I will be first in line. Well, maybe fifth in line, because I know your parents, and grandma, and Marcus will be the first four people."

I smiled. "Well, it's not that. This is hypothetical." I wasn't sure if I should mention Marcus's restaurant idea, since I didn't want Ariana to think he was spending his time at work thinking about planning his own business. Maybe I was overthinking it, but I figured it was better to be safe than sorry. "If someone wanted to open a restaurant, what would they need to do—or have?"

"Money," Ariana said immediately. "It costs a lot of money to open a restaurant. You have to rent space, furnish it, hire kitchen workers and waitstaff. A manager. All that costs money."

"Okay . . ." I knew Marcus didn't have much money at the moment. But I remembered him saying something about getting money from the state since he was an exoneree. I'd have to ask him about that. Maybe part of it could go toward the restaurant.

"What else do you need, besides money?" I asked Ariana.

"You need to get permits and licenses. Of course, you have to come up with a menu."

The menu sounded like it'd be the easiest part. Permits? Licenses? I didn't know about any of that stuff.

"Ariana," Gabe called from the doorway between the kitchen and the front of the bakery. "The camp group just got here."

"Be right there," Ariana told him. To me, she said, "I have to get back to work, but let me know if you have any other questions."

"I will. Thanks!"

She turned to go, but then stopped to look at me again. "Actually, do you want to help with the group? I'll see if Gabe can manage the front alone. I could use an extra set of hands while demoing everything."

"Yes!" The word came out lightning fast.

"Great. Grab an apron and I'll meet you in the party room."

I zipped to the closet, threw on an apron, and waited in the party room with my biggest smile, feeling lucky once more to have my dream job. Well, my dream job for now.

Chapter Five

That night I FaceTimed Marcus. When he answered, all I saw in the phone screen was a close-up of his ear.

"Hey, Little T," he said.

"Hey, Big T. I'm on video."

When he moved the phone so I could see his face, he looked super confused. Then he laughed. "My bad. Got the icons confused. How are you?"

"Great! I wanted to tell you that I asked Ariana some questions about opening a restaurant." I quickly added, "Don't worry, I didn't tell her this was about you."

"It's all good. What'd she have to say?"

"She said what we need the most is money. But aren't you supposed to get money from the state? Since you were wrongfully convicted?"

Marcus's face looked uncertain. "I'm not sure. My lawyer said I'm eligible for exoneree compensation, but he also said it doesn't always come so easily. He sent me this article about how difficult the state is making it for people."

I frowned. "Oh. Can you text the article to me? I want to read it."

"Text it? Uh, sure, one second . . ."

I laughed. "I'll walk you through it."

Once I showed Marcus how to send me the article, I quickly read it. It talked about the Massachusetts wrongful conviction compensation statute, a law that says that people who have been exonerated of a crime can get up to $500,000. My mouth dropped when I read that part.

"Whoa," I said to Marcus, who was still on the FaceTime. "Five hundred thousand dollars is a lot of money! That has to be enough to open a restaurant."

"It's more than enough, but read the rest of the article."

I did. Some of it was confusing, but I got the gist—Massachusetts didn't make it easy to get that money.

"I see," I told Marcus. "But you're still going to try, right?"

"Of course. My lawyer is already working on it, but he told me not to expect compensation anytime soon. That's why I'm grateful for my two jobs. I can build up some savings again."

My mouth twisted as I thought this through. "What about getting a bank loan? Don't people do that when they want to open a business?"

"I'm not sure."

"Can you find out? Maybe ask at the bank?" I asked.

"I'll look into it," Marcus said.

"You promise?"

Marcus laughed. "I promise I will make an appointment at the bank."

"Can I come with you?"

"Okay. But, you know, I think we have more important things to discuss first."

"What?"

He gave me a knowing smile. "The menu. What will we serve at this restaurant? I've been dreaming up recipes in my mind for years. While I was in prison chopping up vegetables for the same stews and rice dishes I helped cook in that kitchen, I was thinking about what I'd cook when I finally got out."

"You can do that now," I said. "You can cook whatever you want."

"Exactly. I was thinking, we should get together and start planning some recipes. Maybe we can do it on Sundays, and then serve Sunday dinner to your parents and grandma. They can give us their opinions on everything."

"That is such a good idea. I can help you cook and make the dessert."

"Okay, think about what you want to make this Sunday. We can go to the grocery store in the morning."

"Sounds like a plan."

Marcus beamed. "You know, growing up, my parents always did Sunday dinner after church," Marcus said. "It'll be nice to get it going again."

I imagined it. My parents, Marcus, Grandma, and I all together every Sunday night, enjoying a yummy meal. One big happy family. I could even put together a Sunday dinner playlist. I felt warm and fuzzy inside just thinking about it.

"I can't wait," I told Marcus. I truly couldn't.

After we said goodbye and hung up, I read the article Marcus had sent one more time. One part stuck out to me. There was a quote from an interview with another man who'd been in prison for twenty-six years. Twenty-six whole years! That was almost double my lifetime so far. He'd been released from prison after the charges against him were finally dropped. But the original conviction was still on his record, and he had a hard time getting a job. He was out of prison, but still struggling to survive.

It didn't seem fair. Was it really justice if he couldn't get back to living a regular life?

I shouldn't have been surprised. I already knew our justice system wasn't fair. If society didn't care about the thousands of people serving prison sentences for crimes they didn't commit, how could I expect them to care about their lives once they finally got out?

More people needed to care. Especially about people of color, who were the ones most affected by this problem.

Marcus was right—he really was one of the lucky ones. I hoped his luck would continue.

Chapter Six

When I knocked on Trevor's door for our movie night, it finally felt like all the past summer nights when the two of us would hang out. I'd changed out of my work uniform and into my comfiest sweatpants and T-shirt. I hadn't even bothered putting on my flip-flops to go over to Trevor's house, since all I had to do was walk out my front door, onto our shared front porch, and into his house. It was eight steps, tops. I carried an armful of snacks, including a chocolate dessert, as promised. As soon as I got home from Ari's Cakes, I'd baked a batch of brownies and I'd also made caramel popcorn from scratch. Trevor's family always had a ton of drink options, so I knew we'd be covered there.

What I hadn't expected was for Maya to already be there when I opened Trevor's door.

"Hey, girl!" Maya said as she walked down the hallway toward me.

We hugged and then I got a better look at her floral sundress, which was pretty, but seemed dressy for movie night. She was wearing makeup, too, and had ditched her glasses for contacts.

"Hey!" I said. "I didn't know you were already here. You look really cute."

She smiled. "Thanks! I felt like wearing a dress. I got here fifteen minutes ago."

"Oh. Okay."

Why didn't she text me when she got here? I thought. *And why didn't she come over to my house first?*

I guessed it wasn't that strange, since the movie night was at Trevor's house, not mine. But it still gave me a weird feeling.

Trevor joined us in the hallway a second later. "Hey, Zoe. Oh, did you make brownies? Sweet!" He grabbed the brownie pan and popcorn bowl from me.

"I added a special ingredient," I said. "You'll see when

you taste them. Hopefully you like it." They were cherry chocolate chip brownies, with cherry halves hidden inside.

"It's a Zoe creation *and* there's chocolate. I'll definitely like it," Trevor said. "My mom also ordered pizza. It should be here soon."

Maya and I followed Trevor into the living room. He set my treats on the coffee table, where there were already three mini water bottles and three soda cans. Trevor sat down on the couch and Maya sat next to him, folding her legs up under her. There wasn't a ton of space left on the couch, so I debated between sitting on the floor or the armchair and chose the armchair.

"What are we watching?" I asked.

"Trevor wants to watch the latest Marvel movie, but there's this musical movie on Netflix that I want to see," Maya said. "Which one do you want? You can be our tiebreaker."

I shrugged. "I'm fine with either."

"We can do the musical movie," Trevor said.

"Yay!" Maya said, grinning. "Thanks, Trev. You're the best."

Trev? I looked at Trevor to see how he'd react to this new nickname.

To my surprise, he looked especially pleased as he turned on the movie.

A few minutes in, I noticed Maya whispering something to Trevor. When she was done, he reached for the yellow throw blanket on his side of the couch and passed it to her. Maya put it over her legs, and I saw her ask if he wanted some of it too.

"I'm cool," he said quietly. "Thanks, though."

They grinned at each other, and I narrowed my eyes. *What's going on here?*

Fifteen minutes later, the doorbell rang. "Probably the pizza," Trevor said, and he paused the movie.

Footsteps came down the stairs. Then I heard Trevor's mom, Patricia, as she paid the pizza delivery person. Trevor got up to help her bring the boxes into the living room.

"Hey, Zoe." Patricia came over and hugged me. "I miss seeing you here all the time. How's your job going?"

"Really great."

"I'm so glad." She turned to Trevor and said, "You're all set here?"

"Yup," Trevor said.

"Okay, enjoy. I'm upstairs if you need anything."

Once Patricia left, we each grabbed slices of pizza and got back to watching the movie.

A while later, after we'd each finished several slices, Trevor grabbed the bowl of popcorn and dropped a large handful into his mouth. "This is good," he said to me.

I smiled. "Thanks."

"Let me try," Maya said. "Here, throw one and I'll catch it."

And then the weirdest thing happened. Maya opened her mouth and Trevor threw a caramel popcorn at it. The first one missed, and she giggled as she picked it up off the couch and ate it. "Mmm!" Trevor tossed a few more until one finally landed in her mouth. They cheered and Maya hugged him.

I sat there, staring at them in horror.

Wait a minute. Do my best friends like each other . . . as more than friends?

As soon as I had the thought, it all made sense. Them texting each other outside of our group. Maya getting here early and dressing up. The way they'd been making googly eyes at each other the whole night.

I'd been the third wheel this whole time, and I hadn't even realized it!

My mind raced. Why hadn't either of them said anything to me? Did they think I wouldn't figure it out?

What did this mean for our friendship? Was this how it would always be now when we hung out?

"Zo? You okay?" Maya asked, knocking me out of my thoughts.

"Um . . ." I froze, not sure what to say—or do. I needed to talk to them about this, but I couldn't do it right then. Maybe I could talk to them separately and get to the bottom of this.

"Actually, I'm not feeling that great," I finally said, realizing I didn't want to sit there watching the two of them act like this for a minute longer. "I think I'm gonna head back home. But you should keep watching the movie. I'll talk to you later."

Maya frowned. "Are you sure? What's wrong?"

"Totally. It's just a headache. I'm sure I'll be fine after I lie down."

"That sucks," Trevor said, sounding sympathetic. "Feel better."

"Thanks. Try the brownies and let me know what you think," I added.

I got up and walked the eight steps back to my house super fast. Then I went straight up to my room and closed the door.

I felt relieved to not be the third wheel at movie night anymore. But that relief quickly disappeared.

What if this changed everything between the three of us forever?

Chapter Seven

I was glad that our first Sunday dinner was that weekend, because I needed the distraction. On Sunday morning, Marcus called to see when I'd be ready to go to the grocery store to pick up the ingredients we needed. He was going to borrow Grandma's car to drive us to the store, so we decided to head over midafternoon.

Baking was the only thing that was going to take my mind off whatever was going on with Trevor and Maya. I still wanted to talk to each of them, but Trevor hadn't been home the day before, and I didn't know how to bring it up when Maya texted to see if I was feeling better.

Today I'd forget about them and focus on baking. But

what should I bake? Not another batch of brownies, and not anything with chocolate, since that would only make me think of Trevor.

I still needed to come up with a signature dessert for our restaurant, but in the meantime, I could make something else that you'd see at a barbecue place. I flipped through a few cookbooks on my shelf to find inspiration and decided on key lime pie with fresh whipped cream. A few years ago, my parents and I had gone on vacation to Key West, Florida, and I'd had the best key lime pie I'd ever tasted. Hopefully I could re-create something just as yummy.

Next, I checked our kitchen cabinets to see what ingredients I was missing. We were going to cook and bake at Grandma's house, so I packed the ingredients I had into a tote bag and wrote down everything else I needed on a Post-it note.

When Marcus arrived in Grandma's car, a Destiny's Child song was playing. Ever since creating my Little Tomato playlist two years earlier after I first exchanged letters with Marcus, the list of songs had grown and grown. It now had hours of music.

"Okay, This or That," I said after we said hello and Marcus started driving toward Wegmans.

This or That was a game Marcus and I had been playing for a while. Even when he was still in prison waiting to see if he'd be exonerated, we'd play it over the phone. The rules were simple—one of us would throw out two options, and the other person would have to say which one they liked better.

"I'm ready," Marcus said.

"Beyoncé in Destiny's Child, or Beyoncé as a solo artist?" I asked.

"That's a tough one," he said. "I mean, Beyoncé as a solo artist is incredible. No question that she's done much better on her own. But I'll always have a soft spot for Destiny's Child." He then sang along to the chorus of "Say My Name," which made me laugh.

"Okay, your turn," I said.

"All right. Chicken or ribs?" he asked.

"Does this have to do with what you're cooking tonight?"

He laughed. "I can't get anything by you. I'm debating between two recipes. I know I made ribs at my birthday party, but I'm thinking of trying a different dry rub seasoning this time. Or, I can do barbecue chicken with my special sauce."

"What's your special sauce?"

"I can't tell you. It's special for a reason."

I acted offended. "You can't even tell your own offspring? Who's about to be your restaurant partner?"

"We'll see, Little T. We'll see . . ."

"Marcus."

He glanced at me before returning his attention to the road. "What?"

"Have you even made this secret sauce before?"

"Hmm, that's the real secret, isn't it?" He chuckled.

"Well, I vote for chicken with secret sauce. If you're still developing it, you should start now." I thought about how it had taken multiple tries to get my Froot Loops cupcake recipe right, and to perfect every other recipe I'd made up since then.

Marcus nodded. "Makes sense."

He pulled into the grocery store lot and parked. "What are you planning to make?"

"Key lime pie and fresh whipped cream. Hopefully they have key limes here."

"Sounds delicious."

"I made a list of the ingredients I need." I took the Post-it out of my pocket and stuck the sticky part to my finger.

Marcus's mouth dropped open. "Wait a second. Did you use paper and pen to write a list? You didn't use your phone? I'm shocked."

I playfully hit his arm. "I wrote actual letters to you, remember?"

"I'm just messing with you. It seems like everyone does everything on their phones nowadays. Except your grandma." He laughed. "Though she still knows technology better than me. She's the one who showed me how to use Netflix. I started binge-watching *Nailed It!*, and it's hilarious."

I giggled. "Let's go inside."

Wegmans was my favorite grocery store. There were so many fresh ingredients everywhere. I especially loved the produce section, where there were tons of delicious fruits that I could bake with. I looked for key limes, and luckily, they had bags of them. Then I went to the baking aisle and got the rest of the ingredients I needed. Marcus got chicken, different seasonings for his "secret sauce," and some potatoes and greens for our sides.

We stood in a check-out line and grinned at each other. I could tell Marcus was just as excited to start cooking as I was to bake. Especially since we'd get to do it together.

Our first Sunday dinner was going to be delicious.

At Grandma's house, we got straight to work. It was four o'clock, so we still had plenty of time before Mom and Dad would come over.

Marcus started mixing up his special sauce so the chicken could marinate. While he did that, I washed my hands and got started on my graham cracker pie crust. I used Grandma's food processer to turn a bunch of graham crackers into crumbs. Then I combined the crumbs with brown sugar and melted butter. I stirred everything with a fork and then used my fingers to combine everything. It felt like digging my fingers in sand.

I scooped some of the mixture into a pie pan. I used a measuring cup to make sure the crumbs made it into all the sides and bottom of the pan. Then I put it into the oven to bake for ten minutes.

When I closed the oven, I saw Marcus taking the chicken he'd bought out of the fridge.

"Did you finish your special sauce?" I asked him. "It smells really good."

"I think so." He put the chicken in a bowl and poured the sauce over it.

I got started on my key lime filling. First, I zested the limes, and then squeezed out all the juice. Then I combined the juice and zest with sweetened condensed milk and yogurt. I used a small spoon to take a tiny taste. It was tangy and yummy. When the graham cracker crust was finished baking, I took it out of the oven. The buttery graham cracker smell filled the air. I poured the key lime filling over it, put the pie back into the oven, and set the timer for fifteen minutes.

The last step was the whipped cream, but I decided to make that closer to dinnertime.

"Do you need any help?" I asked Marcus.

"That'd be great."

For the next hour, I helped him peel and chop potatoes, and he walked me through his potato salad recipe. I also helped him make collard greens. When the food was almost ready, I quickly made a batch of whipped cream and added it to the top of the pie, which I had let cool in the fridge after taking it out of the oven.

"Everything smells delicious," Grandma said as she poked her head into the kitchen. "I'm setting the table with my good china."

"It's not even a special occasion," I told her.

"All of us together with this food is certainly special."

I smiled. "I can help."

Soon after that, my parents came over and we all sat down in the dining room. The food was all in bowls and platters in the center of the table, so we passed them around and served ourselves.

Suddenly I felt nervous. This was the first time all of us were sitting down and eating a meal together. I looked around the table and realized how awkward this night could get.

I knew Mom accepted Marcus and was fine with me

spending time with him. And I knew Marcus had forgiven her for not letting me write to him all those years. But what if things were still tense between them and I just didn't know it?

And what if this was weird for Dad? Lately, I'd been thinking about what life would've been like if Marcus had never gotten accused of a crime. It seemed like Mom and Marcus would've eventually gotten married if he'd never gone to prison. Then Dad might never have become my . . . well, dad. What if Dad thought about that too? I'd think it'd feel strange to share a meal with the person your wife had a kid with and almost married.

There went my appetite. I took a sip of water.

Then Marcus said, "Before we eat, I hope you don't mind if I say a short prayer." We all nodded okay, so he asked all of us to hold hands. I grabbed his left hand, and Grandma held his right. Grandma was next to Mom, Mom was next to Dad, and Dad was next to me. I looked at our held hands, the circle we were forming. We were all connected now—physically, but also in a deeper way. We were all a family now and there was no going back. Everyone else looked peaceful, and maybe a little hungry, while we waited for Marcus to start his prayer.

I took a deep breath and my nerves vanished.

Marcus closed his eyes and thanked God for the food

and this opportunity to all be together. My parents and grandma weren't religious, so I hadn't grown up going to church. Praying wasn't something we usually did before eating. It felt right, though, to give thanks in that moment. Because with all of us together holding hands, I couldn't have felt more grateful.

Chapter Eight

Fourth of July fell on a Monday, and Marcus and I still had to go into work. This holiday was always super busy at Ari's Cakes, because we had lots of cupcakes with patriotic designs that people liked to buy for their Independence Day cookouts.

After work, I was going to watch the local fireworks show with Trevor and our families. Marcus was coming too, since he hadn't seen fireworks in real life since before going to prison. I'd already set aside a dozen of Ariana's Stars and Stripes cupcakes for us to eat while we watched them.

I still wanted to talk to Trevor about Maya, but I didn't

want to do it when our families were around. So as soon as I got home from work, I texted him to see if he wanted to come with me to take Butternut out for a walk. Thankfully he agreed.

I'd thought about what happened at movie night a lot, and realized I'd probably been overreacting. Just because they were being friendly with each other, it didn't mean anything was going on between them. I was close with the two of them, and it only made sense that they'd become close with each other, too. I'd probably freaked out for nothing, but I still wanted to know for sure if anything was going on.

I put Butternut's harness and leash on and went outside. A couple of minutes later, Trevor came out too.

"Hey. Are you feeling better?" Trevor asked. "After movie night?"

"Oh. Yeah. I'm good now. Sorry I left so early."

"It's cool."

"How was the rest of the movie?" I asked.

"Not bad, actually. Some of the songs were pretty catchy."

"Nice."

Butternut pulled his leash, ready to get to walking, so we started down our street. It was hot out, so between that and my nerves around the conversation I was about to have, I started to sweat.

How was I going to bring this up?

I had to just rip the Band-Aid off. "So . . . about you and Maya," I started.

"What about us?" Trevor asked.

"You seemed pretty friendly during movie night."

". . . We're friends."

"Of course. That's what I thought. I just . . . Are you sure it's not . . . more . . . than that? You were acting friendlier than just friends." I looked closely at Trevor to see his reaction to my question.

"What are you asking?" He looked like he was sweating too. I wasn't sure that it was because of the heat.

"C'mon, Trevor. You know what I'm asking." Did I really have to spell it out?

Trevor didn't say anything.

Ugh, I guessed I did. "Do you have a crush on her?" I blurted out.

"What?" He gave a nervous laugh.

I stopped walking, which made Butternut's leash tug, since he was still going. I stared at Trevor, hard. Was he acting nervous because this was a ridiculous assumption, or because I was right?

"You do, don't you?" I finally asked.

"Okay, fine. Yeah." It was like his whole body relaxed after he said the words. "I think I do."

Even though I'd figured it out, I still gasped. "Ahh! Since when?"

Butternut whined, so we started walking again.

"Not long, I swear. Remember when she gave us that update about her dad's surgery a couple of weeks ago? I told my mom about it, and Mom wanted me to pass on her contact info, since she's a nurse. I texted that to Maya. And then I asked how she was doing with everything happening with her dad, and we texted back and forth about that. Then the conversation shifted to other stuff. Now we text every day."

"I had no idea."

"I didn't think this would happen, but she's really easy to talk to." Trevor paused before adding, "And . . . she's pretty."

I had to agree. "She *is* really pretty."

Huh. I wondered if Maya felt the same way as him. But wouldn't I know if she did? When she'd had a crush on Sebastian Walker in the sixth grade, she told me immediately. If she liked Trevor, why was she keeping it a secret from me? Was it because she knew that Trevor and I were close?

Whether she liked him back or not, I still didn't get why Maya hadn't said anything to me about her texts with him.

"Do you think she feels the same way about you?" I asked Trevor.

"I think so?" Trevor looked hopeful. "But I don't know for sure."

"Well . . . are you going to ask her out?"

Trevor shrugged. "I'm thinking about it. Do you think I should? I've never asked a girl out before. And what if I'm wrong and she rejects me?"

Part of me wanted to tell him not to ask her out. If they started dating, it could mess up the friendship that the three of us had together. I really didn't want to be the third wheel every time we all hung out. Not to mention, we were about to start high school and go back to being the youngest in the building. The only thing that made me feel less nervous about it was knowing that Trevor, Maya, and I would go through it together. If they started dating, would I be left all alone?

Still, I knew telling Trevor not to ask Maya out would be selfish. There were two things I was certain about. Trevor was like a brother I never had. And Maya was my best girl friend.

"You are two of my most favorite people," I finally

said. "You should do whatever will make you happy."

Trevor grinned. "Thanks. I think I'm gonna do it. Ask her out." He exhaled. "I hope it goes okay."

"You'll do great," I said. "You could always ask Simon for advice." Simon was Trevor's older brother.

"True. You won't tell Maya we talked about this, right?" he asked. "I'm not sure when I'm going to ask her. I have to find the right time."

"I won't say anything."

"Thanks."

"Okay, new topic," I said. "Let me tell you about this plan me and Marcus have . . ."

I spent the rest of our walk telling Trevor about the restaurant idea. He loved it and asked if he could come to our next Sunday dinner. I said maybe.

But when our walk was over and I was back in my room, I couldn't stop thinking about Trevor and Maya . . . as a couple. If this was really going to happen, I wanted to be mentally prepared.

I knew how Trevor felt about Maya, but now I needed to find out how Maya felt about him.

Chapter Nine

A couple of days later, I still hadn't gotten the chance to talk to Maya about Trevor, but we made plans to hang out on Thursday night after I got home from work. I hoped Trevor wouldn't ask her out before that.

Until then, I decided to focus on planning the restaurant. Marcus made an appointment to talk to a bank about getting a business loan. In the meantime, I was going to keep thinking of a signature dessert. The key lime pie I'd made at our first Sunday dinner had come out amazing. Everyone loved it, and Marcus even went back for seconds. It could totally be on our restaurant menu, but I still didn't think it was special enough to become a signature dessert.

While I worked behind the counter at Ari's Cakes, my brain turned with other possible ideas. A trio of mini donuts with different dipping sauces? A fancy chocolate mousse? Maybe I could ask Marcus what his favorite dessert of all time was and come up with a twist to make it even better.

"What can I get for you?" I asked the next person in line, a girl who looked around my age.

"Are you Zoe?" she asked, tucking her short blond hair behind her ears.

"Oh. Um, yeah." I had been expecting to hear a cupcake order, not my name. I wasn't even wearing a name tag. "Do I know you?"

She shook her head. "I don't think so. I'm Hannah Morrison. It's . . . nice to meet you." She looked at the people in line behind her. "Do you have a break or something soon?"

I glanced at the clock on the wall. "Yeah, in forty-five minutes."

She smiled. "Okay. I'll wait. I wanted to talk to you about something, if that's okay."

"Oh. Um. Sure. Okay." *A total stranger wants to talk to me? What could this be about?*

"Great! In the meantime, I'll take a . . ." She glanced at

the cupcake display. "S'mores cupcake. And a small lemonade."

"Sure." I grabbed the cupcake for her and put it on a plate. Then I filled a cup with ice and our house-made lemonade. She paid and I watched as she sat at one of the empty tables by the window. She took her phone and a book out of her backpack.

What's going on? I couldn't spend a lot of time thinking about it because the next customer was ready to order.

Fifteen minutes before my break was supposed to start, there were no new customers. "I'm going to take my break a few minutes early, if that's okay with you," I told Gabe. By this point, Hannah had finished her cupcake and lemonade, used the bathroom, and had read through many pages of her book. I was ready to get to the bottom of why she was here, and how she knew my name.

"Fine with me," he said.

As soon as I came out from behind the counter, Hannah saw me and put her book away. "Sorry if that was weird," she said. "The way I just said your name like that. I could tell I freaked you out. I thought you must get that a lot."

I sat down across from her. "Get what a lot?"

"Random people coming to talk to you."

"Why would random people come talk to me?"

"Because of your story."

My face must've been full of confusion, because she said, "I heard your interview on Boston Public Radio. And then I read the articles about Marcus's case. How you helped find his alibi witness. I heard you say in the radio interview that you worked here, so I came by to see you."

Ohhh, I thought. That explained how she knew my name, but what did she want to talk to me about?

"My mom is in prison," Hannah blurted out next. "Not my whole life, not like Marcus. But she's been in and out a lot."

"Oh," I said. "I'm sorry."

"I don't really have anyone to talk to about it," Hannah said. "I mean, there's my dad and my brother, but sometimes I wish I had a friend my age to talk to. My friends at school don't understand what it's like. None of their parents are in prison."

I nodded. "I know what you mean. My best friends knew my birth dad was in prison, but I barely talked to them about it. They didn't even know what his crime was at first. It felt easier to *not* talk about it."

"Exactly!" she said. "Anyway, I know my situation is a little different because Marcus was innocent of his crime,

64

and he's out now. My mom . . ." Her voice got lower. "She's not innocent." Then she quickly added, "She's not a monster! Her crimes are all drug-related, like she was caught with drugs. Usually, she ends up in prison for a while, and when she gets out, she'll agree to go to rehab. I start thinking things will be better, and she starts acting more like a mom to me again. But then she ends up back on drugs, gets arrested again, and it's this whole horrible cycle. I finally realized she's never going to change."

"That sounds really hard."

"When I heard you on the radio . . . My dad was listening to it. He listens to Boston Public Radio all the time, and usually it's super boring. But when your interview came up, I got excited because I don't know any other kids who've had a parent in prison. So, I came here to see you. I hope I don't seem like a stalker! I promise, this is the first time I've done anything like this."

I laughed. "No, it's fine! I'm glad you came by. Even though Marcus is out now, I know exactly how you feel."

Hannah looked relieved. She started to say something else, but then her phone buzzed. "Ugh. That's my dad. He dropped me off but said I could only stay for an hour. I have to go, but can we talk more later? Maybe we can hang out sometime?"

I grinned. "Sure. I'd love to."

Hannah looked thrilled. We exchanged phone numbers so we could text each other.

For the rest of the workday, I kept thinking about how random, but cool, it was that Hannah found me through the Boston Public Radio interview. It made me feel good that my story helped her feel less alone. And she seemed really nice. I was excited to get to know her.

Marcus had said he also got emails and letters, through his lawyers, after our radio interview and the other local news stories that had come out after his release. He was inspiring people with his story, too, especially other innocent inmates.

The more I thought about it, the more I realized how fun it was to be on the radio, to have people around the city hear my voice and my story. I wished I could do it again. It especially made me feel hopeful about Marcus and I opening a restaurant. We were a feel-good story now! People would want to see us succeed. Maybe we could do a follow-up interview once our restaurant was open. Then people would line up to come eat our food.

Our future—mine and Marcus's—looked bright. Nothing could stand in our way.

Chapter Ten

After work on Thursday, Grandma dropped me off at Maya's house so we could hang out. Standing outside of Maya's front door, I felt jittery all over. I had no idea what would happen when I asked her about Trevor, but I hoped everything would still be the same between us.

Maya's mom opened the door after I rang the doorbell. "Hi, sweetie," she said.

"Hi! I brought over some extra cupcakes from work." I held up a box of six cupcakes. They were assorted flavors: one cookies 'n' cream, one strawberry shortcake, one banana nut, one tie-dye surprise (the surprise was cookie butter filling), one vanilla with chocolate frosting, and one chocolate with vanilla frosting.

Maya's mom took the box from me. "That's so nice of you! Let me go ahead and hide these from Grace, though, so she doesn't ask for any before dinner." Grace was Maya's younger sister.

"Good idea," I said.

Maya appeared at the top of the stairs. "Hey! Come on up."

I followed Maya up to her room and sat down on her bed while she shut the door. Her bed was so comfortable. It had the fluffiest comforter and a bunch of extra pillows all over. It felt like lying down on a cloud.

On her desk were a bunch of art supplies and stickers. "What are you making?" I asked.

"Some cards for my friends at camp. Since I won't get to see them this summer, I'm making them collages to hang up in their bunks. I want to send them a care package, too." Then Maya said, "Oh! Can you help me bake some cookies to send them?"

"Sure!" I went over and looked at the collages Maya had made so far. They had a mix of quotes, photos from magazines, and pictures of Maya and her camp friends. "These are so nice. Are you sad you aren't at camp right now?" Maya's aunt and uncle ran the sleepaway camp in Western Massachusetts, so I couldn't remember a summer when she hadn't gone.

"Yeah. Especially since this would've been my last summer to be a regular camper. Next year I'll become a CIT."

"What does CIT mean?" I asked.

"Counselor-in-training. But that'll still be fun. And it's worth it to be here for my dad this summer."

"How's your dad doing?" I hadn't seen him downstairs in the living room, where he often was when I came over. Maya had mentioned that he'd been sleeping more lately.

Maya sighed. "He's doing okay. His surgery is next week."

"Are you nervous?"

"A little. But his pre-op appointments are going well. My mom says I don't need to worry about anything. Of course, I am, though. How can I not?"

"Right. Totally. I hope everything goes okay."

"Thanks."

We both got quiet, but it wasn't the awkward kind of quiet. That's what I loved about being around Maya. We could be silent with each other and still feel normal.

Except this time, it was a little different because there was a big elephant in the room: Trevor.

While Maya picked up her glue stick and attached

another picture to one of her collages, I thought about how to bring him up. Now that I knew Trevor liked her, it felt like I was holding on to this huge secret.

"Did you have fun at movie night, after I left?" I finally asked.

Maya looked up from her desk. "Oh my gosh, your brownies were sooo good. I think Trevor ate like three of them. Maybe we should make those for my care package. Since everyone always gets cookies."

"I'm glad you liked them." I paused, and then said, "So . . . what did you and Trevor talk about after I left?"

Maya shrugged. "We mostly just watched the movie."

Hmm.

"What do you think of Trevor? You two never usually hang out without me there."

"I know," Maya said. "He's a nice guy."

"Do you think he's . . . cute?" It felt strange to ask this about Trevor, who was like a member of my family. He was practically my brother. But as soon as the question was out, I knew my answer because Maya's cheeks turned bright red.

"You do, don't you?" I asked.

"I mean, don't *you*?" Maya asked. "Lots of people think he's cute."

"They do? Who?"

Maya shrugged. "Other kids at school."

"I guess I've never looked at him that way before."

"That's because you two are too close," Maya said.

"Does this mean you have a crush on him?" I asked.

Maya looked down at her lap. "Don't hate me."

"Why would I hate you?"

"Because I don't want things to be weird between us. He's been your friend this whole time." She looked up at me. "But yeah, I like him."

"Wow." I forced a smile, but my stomach flip-flopped. This was really happening. My two best friends liked each other, as more than just friends. I knew it, and it was only a matter of time before they knew it, too.

"You're okay with this?" Maya asked.

"I mean, sure," I said, even though I wasn't totally sure.

Maya looked relieved. "I'm *so* glad. Honestly, I've wanted to tell you about this for weeks, but I didn't know how to bring it up."

"Weeks?"

"Yeah. Trevor and I have been texting. Just as friends, but I don't know. Maybe it could become something more. I wish I had an older sibling to talk to about this, because I have no idea what to do next."

"Don't look at me," I said, laughing nervously.

I'd had crushes before, but nothing ever came of them. I wasn't even completely sure I'd wanted anything to come of them. I figured I'd get my first boyfriend sometime in high school. But now high school was almost here.

Maya sat next to me on her bed. "Do you think Trevor could like me back? I don't think he's texting with other girls. Except for you, of course."

Should I tell her what Trevor told me? But I'd told him that I wouldn't say anything until he was ready to ask her out. I didn't want to lie to Maya, but I also really didn't want to be in the middle of all of this.

Why, of all the kids in our town, did they have to have crushes on *each other*?

"I don't know," I said, hoping Maya couldn't tell I was lying.

Maya sighed. "I guess I'll keep talking to him and see what happens."

I nodded.

"I'm glad you know now." Maya lay back in her bed, looking totally relaxed and relieved. "I hated keeping this secret from you."

But now I was keeping a secret from her. I kinda hoped Trevor would ask her out soon, so it would all be out in the open. But things would change between the three of us. How could I do movie nights with them without feeling like a third wheel? Would they even *want* me to be part of movie nights anymore?

What if they started going out and only wanted to hang out with each other from now on?

A huge lump settled in my stomach.

What if this meant I was going to lose my two best friends?

Chapter Eleven

As soon as my mom picked me up from Maya's house, I sent Trevor a text.

ME: You'll tell me before you ask Maya out, right?

I watched to see if three dots would appear to show that Trevor was typing, but nothing happened. I clicked back to my list of text convos. The one right below that was the one between me and Hannah. There was only one message so far—Hannah saying it was her, from when we exchanged numbers.

If I was about to lose my two best friends, this could

be a good time to get to know Hannah. Plus, I really liked talking to her. I started typing.

ME: Hey it's Zoe

I pressed Send, and this time, the three dots immediately appeared. A second later, she replied.

HANNAH: Zoe! Hi! 👋
ME: I still can't get over that you tracked me down after hearing me on the radio
HANNAH: I know right? I've never done anything like that before.
ME: 😊
HANNAH: Though to be fair you DID say to come by Ari's Cakes
ME: True
HANNAH: Do you wanna FaceTime?
ME: I'll be home in 5 min. I'll call you then

When I got to my room, I FaceTimed Hannah and she answered right away. I couldn't see too much of her background, but she was sitting against a pillow, so I guessed she was in her bedroom too.

"Hey," she said. "My dad is making me fold my

75

laundry and put it away, so this way I can talk to you at the same time." She set the phone down on her nightstand so it faced her.

Now I could see more of her room. Her bed was pushed against the wall, which was lined with Broadway posters from *Wicked*, *The Lion King*, *Waitress*, and *Hamilton*.

"I'm guessing you're into musicals," I said.

Hannah glanced at the wall behind her. "I'm obsessed. Look." She picked up her phone again and turned the camera so I could see the rest of her walls. They all had Broadway posters. "I also have a *Playbill* collection."

"That's awesome," I said when she put the phone back down. "Do you like performing in them too?"

"Oh, no, I only like watching them. You don't want to hear me sing."

I laughed.

Hannah picked up two socks from the clothes pile in front of her and balled them together.

"By the way, where do you live?" I asked. I didn't think she lived in the same town as me, since I'd never seen her before.

"Newton," she said.

That town wasn't all that far away.

"What about you?" she asked.

"Medford."

"Cool." She paused and then said, "Do you mind if I ask more questions about your dad being in prison? I mean, what it was like for you? We didn't get to talk long at the bakery."

"Oh. Sure," I said.

Hannah smiled and looked relieved. "Thanks. But, I mean, if you don't want to share something, that's fine too."

"I don't mind," I said. And I didn't. It was different, knowing that Hannah was going through something similar. It made me feel like I could be more open.

"Okay. So, what was it like, growing up without your dad?" Hannah asked.

"Well, my mom got married to my stepdad when I was little, so I always felt like I had a dad. Now it's like I have two dads, except I'm still getting to know Marcus. That's what I still call him—Marcus. Or sometimes Big T. That stands for Big Tomato . . . It's a long story." I was rambling, but Hannah didn't seem to mind.

"Do you ever want to call Marcus 'Dad'?" she asked. "Since he's your biological father?"

I'd thought about this since Marcus got out of prison. If I'd been able to talk to him my whole life, I probably would've called him Dad from the start. And when Mom got married, I probably would've had a different name for my stepdad. Like, maybe he'd be Paul to me. But that felt weird. There was no way I could start calling him Paul now. Could I call them both Dad?

I shrugged. "So far, no. But maybe I will one day. I'm not sure."

"That makes sense." Then Hannah said, "My dad hasn't gotten remarried. He's dating someone now, though. Her name's Erica. She's nice, but sometimes she's too nice. Like she's trying too hard. Sometimes I mention my mom's name when she's around just to make her cringe."

I gave a small laugh, but then got serious again. "How long is your mom going to be in prison?"

"She gets out in eighteen months. It's a two-year sentence." Hannah exhaled loudly. "But I'm not really talking to her right now."

"Why not?"

"Because she doesn't keep any of her promises! It's so frustrating. Last year, she swore to me that she'd get clean for real and be there for me and my brother. But then she ended up getting arrested again. I'm tired of going through this every few months. Sometimes I wish I was more like you, and never knew her."

I almost gasped. "You don't mean that. She's your mom."

Hannah rolled her eyes. "She gave birth to me. That's

about it." She stopped folding laundry, and suddenly looked sad. She turned away from the camera and wiped her eyes.

"I'm sorry," I told her, not sure what else to say. What would I do without my mom? I guessed I was lucky. Even though I hadn't gotten to have Marcus in my life until recently, I had two parents at home to love me. And Marcus cared about me, even when he was locked up. He'd still loved me.

Hannah shook her head, like she was trying to shake all her sadness away. "Thanks. I could never admit that to my other friends. They wouldn't understand."

"They might surprise you." I thought of Trevor and Maya and how supportive they'd been when I finally opened up to them about Marcus. "But if you want to talk to me about this stuff again, or anything else, let me know."

Hannah smiled. "I'd like that."

Right then a notification popped up on my screen. A new text.

TREVOR: I think I'm gonna tell Maya I like her on Saturday. Wish me luck.

I swiped away the notification, but my whole body went cold.

"What is it?" Hannah asked, looking worried.

My face must've changed. "Oh, um, just a text from my friend Trevor."

"Is everything okay? You looked like someone'd died all of a sudden."

Our trio is dying, I thought. *It's only a matter of time now.*

"Everything's fine. Sort of. Trevor was telling me that he's going to ask out our other friend, Maya. I already know she'll say yes because she told me she likes him back."

"Ohh," Hannah said, like this was a juicy piece of gossip. If they weren't my best friends, I'd act the same way.

"I don't know how I feel about it. Like, I don't want to lose either of them, you know?"

"Do you think they'll stop being your friends just because they like each other?" Hannah asked.

"No, but I'm worried it could happen even if they don't mean for it to. Like they'll start spending so much time with each other, and have no time left for me."

And I'll spend the rest of this summer alone. And then start high school alone, I thought but didn't say out loud.

"Have you gone out with anyone yet?" I asked. "Or have any of your friends?"

"Some of my friends have," Hannah said. "And I've had a crush before. This . . . well, this girl in my dance class who's really cute." Hannah was looking at me like she wasn't sure how I'd react to that.

"That's cool," I said. "Do you think she liked you back?"

Hannah smiled a little. "I don't know. But that's okay. I'm not sure I'm ready to go out with anyone yet."

"Same here, honestly," I said.

"Well, when your friends go out, let me know and we can hang out," Hannah said. "Do you ever do facial masks?"

I shook my head. "I've seen them at the store, but I've never done one before."

"They're my favorite way to relax—besides listening to Broadway music. I'll bring some when we get together."

"Okay. That sounds fun."

Hannah and I grinned at each other.

When we ended our FaceTime, I opened Trevor's text again. As I typed, I pretended to be excited.

ME: Ahh good luck! Let me know what happens!
TREVOR: Will do

I put my phone down and hoped this didn't turn out to be a disaster. For any of us.

81

Chapter Twelve

"*Did a hurricane blow through* here?"

I turned away from my closet to find Dad standing in my doorway. He looked confused, which made sense since my clothes were all over the floor. I'd spent the last half hour pulling things out of my closet and drawers, trying to figure out what to wear. Marcus and I had an appointment at a bank today to find out if we were eligible for a business loan for our restaurant. I wanted to "dress to impress," as Grandma liked to say.

"What should I wear to a bank meeting?" I asked.

Recognition flashed in Dad's eyes. "Is this about the restaurant?"

"Yup. I know the loan we're asking about will be under Marcus's name, but it'll still be my restaurant, too. I want to look professional so the banker will take me seriously."

Nodding, Dad came over to my closet. "Hmm, let's see here." He flipped through the clothes still on my hangers, and then picked through the pile on the floor.

"How about this?" He held up the black-and-white striped dress that I'd worn to my eighth-grade awards ceremony a month earlier.

I stared at the dress and nodded. "That could work. Thanks!"

He passed it to me. "Anytime, kiddo. Good luck today."

I put on the dress and pulled my hair into a simple ponytail. Then I grabbed my pair of black flats before heading outside.

When Marcus arrived in Grandma's car, which he had borrowed again, I saw that I wasn't the only one who wanted to dress to impress. He was wearing a pair of khakis and a blue button-down shirt.

"You look nice, Little T," he said when he saw me.

"So do you." I smiled, suddenly having a good feeling about today. We looked great. Our restaurant idea was great. *We* were great. The bank had to see that.

When we got there, we sat down in the waiting area.

"Mr. Johnson?" a woman asked a few minutes later. She wore a pair of navy pants and a white blouse, and had a name tag that said "Sheila Richards, Loan Officer."

"Yes, that's me." Marcus stood up and reached out to shake her hand. "You can call me Marcus. This is my daughter, Zoe."

"I'm also his business partner," I added.

Sheila smiled as she shook Marcus's hand, and then mine. "Nice to meet you both. I'm Sheila. Come on back."

Marcus and I followed her to her office, which was a partitioned area in the back corner of the bank. She sat behind her desk, and we sat on the two chairs across from her.

Sheila folded her hands together on her desk. "I reviewed the information you sent me. Unfortunately, we're not going to be able to extend you a loan at this time."

"Wait, what? Why?" I blurted out.

Marcus gave me a look that said, "Give her a chance to explain."

Sheila shook her head. "I'm sorry. Marcus, you don't meet our requirements. Your credit score is low because you have no recent credit history."

"What's that?" I whispered to Marcus.

"It's like a record showing I'm responsible with my money," Marcus whispered back. "That I pay my bills on time. But I haven't had any bills to repay while in prison, so now I don't have that record."

I nodded at him as Sheila continued.

"You also don't have much work history, due to your . . . past." It was obvious she didn't want to say the word "prison." "But you're employed now, so that's great. If you can build some credit and get your score up, you might be eligible for a loan at a later time."

"Okay. I understand," Marcus said.

Wait. "That's it?" I asked Marcus, forgetting to whisper this time. "You're going to accept this?"

"We have to," Marcus said to me. To Sheila, he said, "Thank you for your time."

Marcus stood up and I did the same.

"I'm sorry it's not better news." Sheila handed him her business card. "Feel free to reach out if you have any other questions. Or, if you want, I can have my colleague help you open a credit card?"

"You know, I'll come back another time for that," Marcus said. "Thank you, though."

We said goodbye and I followed Marcus back through the bank lobby to the exit. When we got outside, the sun shone so bright, both of us had to shield our eyes to walk across the parking lot to Grandma's car. We got inside and put our seat belts on, but Marcus didn't turn on the car right away.

He looked at me. "I'm sorry."

"Why are you sorry?" I gave a frustrated sigh. "It's not your fault. It's like that article you sent me. People should be willing to give you a chance, after all you've been through."

"No," Marcus said, and I glanced at him, confused. "I mean, I'm sorry for getting your hopes up. I should've kept my mouth shut about this restaurant. I knew it probably wouldn't be able to happen anytime soon. I'm still getting back on my feet."

"I'm glad you told me," I said. "I'm glad we're doing this."

"Me too. It just might take longer than we thought," Marcus said. "I want you to be prepared for that."

"How long?" I asked.

"Long enough for me to get my finances in order. I'm basically starting from scratch. I have a new bank account, but no savings yet. I should probably get a credit card, too, so I can prove to the bank that I can pay a bill on time. It's good that I have these two jobs, but it'll take time for my credit to build up. Maybe even years."

Years? My heart sank.

"Can't we go to another bank?" I asked. "Maybe a different bank would have different criteria."

"We can try." But Marcus didn't look too positive. "My lawyer warned me about this, and said it happens a lot with his clients. They get out of prison, their records get cleared, but they still have trouble doing regular things, like getting a loan."

"Don't you see how unfair this is? If you hadn't been wrongfully convicted, you *would* have your finances in order already. It shouldn't have to be like this!"

"If I've learned anything over the years," Marcus said. "It's that the way that the world *should* be and the way it *is* are two separate things."

For a moment, neither of us spoke. I didn't know what else to say.

"We should get going," Marcus said. "My shift at Ari's Cakes starts soon."

"Okay." I didn't have to work today, so I was ready to go home and change into more comfortable clothes.

Marcus squeezed my knee. "Don't worry. We will open a restaurant eventually. We just have to be patient."

Patience was not one of my strengths. It hadn't been

when it came to finding out the truth about Marcus's conviction, and it wasn't now.

We had to be able to do something, so we didn't have to wait years to open Marcus's dream restaurant.

But what?

Chapter Thirteen

Disappointment weighed on me during the car ride home. Marcus turned on the Little Tomato playlist and "No Scrubs" by TLC played. That song usually put me in a good mood, but not this time. It was just a reminder that we wouldn't get to listen to the playlist in our very own restaurant kitchen anytime soon.

Sheila said the bank would reconsider when Marcus got his finances in order, but what if that wasn't true? What if Marcus's time in prison would always be held against him?

When I got home, I went straight to my room to change into shorts and a T-shirt. My clothes from earlier were still all over the place, but I was in no mood to clean.

Only one thing could get me out of this funk. I decided to bake all my frustrations out.

I was walking downstairs toward the kitchen when I heard voices come in through the open window in the living room.

I recognized them immediately and froze. It was Trevor and Maya.

Had Maya already been here when I got home, or had she come over while I was upstairs? Either way, I wasn't sure if I should go outside and say hi. She was clearly only here to see Trevor, since she hadn't told me she was coming or that she was here.

What if Trevor had already asked her out? Then I definitely didn't want to go outside.

But he'd said he'd tell me how it went. I checked my phone. No texts yet—from either of them.

OMG. Was Trevor about to ask Maya out *right now?*

I tiptoed into the living room and sat down low on the couch so I couldn't be seen from outside. Butternut immediately came over and licked my hand.

"Shh," I told him, and focused on listening.

"Tomorrow we're having this family day," Maya was saying.

"What's that?" Trevor asked.

"My grandparents are coming over and we're going to play games and eat food together."

"That sounds fun."

"Yeah." Maya sighed. "It just makes me nervous about the surgery. Like, are they having a party now because they're worried my dad won't be able to do those things afterward?"

Maya's dad's surgery was on Tuesday. I put it on the calendar on my phone so I wouldn't forget to text Maya to check in.

"I get it," Trevor said. "But my mom said the hospital he's going to is one of the best. And he's in good hands."

"Yeah."

There was silence for a few seconds.

"So, um, I wanted to ask you something," Trevor said.

Ahh, it's happening! I leaned in closer to the window.

"What?" Maya asked.

Trevor cleared his throat. "Actually, are you thirsty? I'm gonna grab a soda. Do you want one?"

"Sure."

I heard Trevor go inside his house. For a second, I debated going outside to say hi to Maya. Trevor probably wouldn't ask Maya out in front of me. Maybe I could stop this entire thing from happening.

But no. That would be totally selfish. If they wanted

to go out, they should. And it wasn't like Trevor wouldn't find another time to ask her.

I had to accept this, even if it meant my friendship with the two of them would completely change.

Butternut licked my hand again. "At least I still have you, Nutter Butter," I whispered to him.

Just then my phone vibrated. I took it out of my pocket and read the text.

MAYA: Hey! Are you home?

I stared at it. *What should I say?* It wouldn't be selfish to answer honestly and say that I was home. But then she'd probably come in to say hi. Now that I knew Trevor was most likely building up the courage to ask her out, I felt bad ruining the moment for him.

It was only a tiny lie. I didn't think it would hurt anyone.

ME: Nope! Still out with Marcus. Why?

I guessed this meant I was stuck here until Maya went inside Trevor's house or headed back home.

MAYA: No reason. Chat later?

I frowned at my phone screen. Why didn't Maya just tell me that she was over at Trevor's? Did she not want me to know?

Ugh. This was exactly what I was worried about. Shaking my head, I typed out my response.

ME: definitely!

Trevor came back outside, and I heard two soda cans opening.

"What were you going to ask me?" Maya asked.

I shifted positions on the couch so I could peek outside the window. If either of them looked closely, they might have been able to see me, but they were both sitting on the top step, facing the street. I was safe to eavesdrop.

Maybe it was wrong, but I had to see this.

"Oh. Right," Trevor said. He rubbed the back of his neck, like he was sweaty or something. "Well, I was thinking maybe we could, like, hang out sometime. Like, not here, but, I don't know, at a restaurant. Or the movies."

"Just the two of us?" Maya asked.

Trevor nervously laughed. "Yeah. Just us."

I wished I could see their faces, but all I could do was read their body language from behind.

Maya tucked her hair behind her ear and said, "Okay.

I'd like that." She sounded like she was smiling.

"For real?" Trevor cleared his throat again. "I mean, great." He took a sip of his soda, but when he put it down, his hands must've been shaky, because it tipped over. Soda started spilling out onto the porch.

"Shoot!" Trevor said as he and Maya stood up quickly to avoid getting soda on them. "Sorry."

"It's okay," Maya said.

"I'll go get some paper towels."

"I can help."

The two of them got up and went inside.

I sat up on the couch. I'd heard enough of their conversation.

Maya and Trevor were going out.

It was okay. I was happy for them. This would be fine.

I walked into the kitchen and automatically started taking flour and sugar out of the cabinet, even though I didn't know what recipe I was making. But then I realized I didn't feel like baking anymore.

When Maya told me the next day that she had big news and wanted to FaceTime, I pretended not to know what it could be.

There was a lot of background noise when she first called.

"Hold on, my family's all here, but they're putting the food out and stuff." Maya carried her phone up the stairs and into her bedroom. Once she closed the door, she said, "I wanted to talk last night, but I didn't get the chance. You'll never guess what happened."

"What?" Of course, I already knew. Not only because I'd witnessed the whole thing, but Trevor had also messaged me last night. He asked me to meet him on the porch, where he gave me the whole rundown of what'd happened. Including the part where he spilled the soda.

"Oh no!" I'd said to him, pretending to be surprised. "What happened next?"

I had to admit—it made me happy to see Trevor look so happy. Now I'd get to hear the entire story from Maya's point of view. She beamed as she told me.

"That's so exciting!" I said.

"I know! I think we're going to hang out next Saturday. By then Dad should be home recovering."

"Did you tell your parents?"

"Not yet," Maya said. "Do you think they'll believe we're still only friends? I kind of don't want to tell them yet."

"Yeah. They'll be distracted anyway."

"You have to help me pick out what to wear."

"Okay." Then I said, "I think I'll hang out with Hannah that night."

"Who's Hannah?"

I'd forgotten I hadn't told Maya about Hannah yet, so I told her everything that'd happened when Hannah came to see me at Ari's Cakes.

"I can't believe she found you from the radio interview!" Maya said when I was done.

"I know, right?"

She laughed. "You're totally famous."

"Not famous enough." I filled her in on the bank situation, how Marcus and I weren't going to be able to get a loan. "Without that money, we have to put the whole restaurant idea on hold."

"That stinks," Maya said. "But maybe there's another way to make it happen."

"Maybe."

Maya looked away from the camera. "That's my mom. They're all set up downstairs. I have to go."

"Have fun with your family."

After we hung up, I texted Hannah to see if she was free the following Saturday night. She said she was.

At least I had one thing to look forward to.

Chapter Fourteen

"Want to go to J.P. Licks with me?" Dad asked that afternoon when I was hanging out in my room. "I could go for a scoop of their red velvet cake ice cream. It's my new favorite flavor."

"I'd love to," I said. "But I have to get ready for Sunday dinner. Marcus and I are going to the grocery store to buy our ingredients." That morning I'd decided to make beignets with two dipping sauces: chocolate and caramel.

"Right," Dad said. "I almost forgot about Sunday dinner."

Now I felt bad. "Can we go one day after work this week instead?"

"Sure thing, kiddo," Dad said, and started to leave.

"Dad?"

He turned around.

"You're okay with me hanging out with Marcus, right?"

"Of course I am," he quickly said. "You have a lot to catch up on. And this new Sunday dinner tradition—it's great. All the food last week was delicious." He smiled, but it seemed kind of forced.

"Okay . . ." I said. "Just making sure."

He flashed another smile before walking out.

I couldn't tell if he was being completely honest with me. But he was right—Marcus and I *did* have a lot of catching up to do. Years of stories to tell. I just had to make sure I still found time to hang out with Dad.

Dinner that night was fried shrimp with a lemon aioli, homemade coleslaw, and grilled corn on the cob. My beignets came out perfectly crispy on the outside and fluffy on the inside. Of course, I had to taste-test a few as I was making them. They looked pretty, too, like little powdered sugar–covered clouds.

Marcus blessed the food and we all dug in.

"How are things going with your jobs?" Mom asked Marcus.

"They've been great. I'm so happy I have both of them. My next plan is to save up for my own place."

"In the meantime, you can stay as long as you need," Grandma said with a smile. "There's always a place for you here. Especially if you keep cooking meals like this." She let out a big mm-hmm, and we all laughed.

"I appreciate that," Marcus said.

"I'm sure it'll be nice to have your own place, though, at some point," Dad said.

"Absolutely. I emailed my lawyer again about the wrongful conviction compensation. I want to see if we can make the process go any faster."

I perked up at that. "If you get the money sooner, we can also use it for the restaurant!"

"You'd probably want to get settled into your own place before you start trying to open your own business, though, right?" Mom asked.

"That would make sense," Dad said.

Wait a second. Were they suddenly *against* the restaurant now?

"I'll have to see," Marcus said, which made me feel a little better. If the state gave Marcus a lot of money, there'd be no reason he couldn't move out *and* open a restaurant at the same time.

"It'd be nice to get started with helping people,"

Marcus said. "That's one of my goals with this restaurant, to be able to help some of the other people who got out of prison and can't find a job."

I looked around the table to see everyone's reactions to that. I still hadn't mentioned this part to my parents. Dad paused eating to look at Marcus, and Mom looked like she was about to say something.

Grandma beat her to it. "How would you help?" she asked.

"I'd hire them. They could be waitstaff, kitchen staff, whatever. I really want to give people who are looking for a fresh start a chance. Like people have done for me."

"That's very generous of you," Grandma said.

"Hold on. You want to hire ex-cons?" Dad asked.

"Not everyone in prison is guilty," I told Dad, stating the obvious.

"That's true, kiddo," Dad said.

"I wouldn't discriminate," Marcus said. "Guilty or innocent, if they spent time in prison and want to build a better life for themselves once they're out, I want to help."

Across the table, I saw Dad give Mom a look, like he wasn't sure about this.

Mom said, "Well, if Zoe's going to be part of this restaurant, we'll just make sure everyone who works there is safe for her to be around."

"I agree," Dad said.

"Of course," Marcus said. "I'd never do anything to put Zoe in danger. I hope you know that."

"Of course you wouldn't," Grandma said.

"I know that, Marcus," Mom said.

From the look on his face, Dad still seemed skeptical. Was it because he didn't believe Marcus, or because he was still uncomfortable with the idea of Marcus hiring former convicts?

Because the truth was, I was still uncomfortable with it too.

Now, if we opened this restaurant, there was a chance my parents wouldn't want me to work there, depending on who Marcus hired.

Maybe I could convince Marcus not to hire people who'd been in prison. At least not ones who'd been guilty. I'd talk to him about it the next time we were alone.

The dining room got quiet, the only sounds the clanking of forks against Grandma's china. It was such a contrast to our first Sunday dinner, where everyone had seemed to enjoy each other's company. Now, the tension in the room was as thick as a block of cold butter.

"Let's talk about something else," Grandma finally said. "Zoe, are you excited to start high school in the fall?"

I shrugged. "I guess. It was nice to be the oldest ones at our school last year. Now I'll be one of the youngest."

"But you'll still have Trevor and Maya," Mom said. "And your other friends."

I hoped that was true. That if Trevor and Maya worked out as a couple, we'd all still be as close, and I'd still be able to rely on them.

Why did the future have to feel so uncertain?

Chapter Fifteen

During my lunch break a couple of days later, I texted Maya in our group chat to see how her dad's surgery had gone. I knew it'd been first thing that morning. Maya didn't respond right away, so she was probably still at the hospital with her family. I hoped everything had gone okay.

Trevor sent a text too.

TREVOR: Thinking about you 💜

I stared at the message. Had Trevor ever used a heart emoji before? No. He hadn't. The closest was the heart eyes emoji, when I shared a picture of a chocolate cheese-cake I'd made once.

Maybe it was time to end this group chat . . .

When I went back to work, I kept my phone in my pocket so I wouldn't miss when Maya texted back. I wasn't supposed to have my phone with me while I was working, but I figured I could sneak a peek if I felt it vibrate in my pocket.

"What can I get for you?" I asked the next person in line.

The woman pushed her huge sunglasses up to the top of her head and said, "I need fifty cupcakes that say, 'Congrats Laura and Brian,' and I need them by five o'clock today."

"Today?" I repeated, not because I hadn't heard her, but because it was such short notice.

"Isn't that what I just said?" The woman scowled at me.

"You did, but, um." I glanced at the clock on the wall behind me. It was 1:36 p.m. "I'm not sure that's possible. Usually, we need forty-eight-hour notice for custom cupcakes."

"Well, this is an unusual situation." She exhaled. "My best friend Laura is getting engaged. I thought it was happening next week, but it's tonight. Her soon-to-be fiancé confirmed this morning. I need these cupcakes to be ready for the surprise engagement party."

"Got it. I'm just not sure—"

"Where is the manager?" she interrupted, her voice rising as she looked around. "Can I speak to them?"

Ugh. I stopped myself from rolling my eyes at her and went over to Gabe. He was at the other end of the counter ringing someone up at the register.

"Excuse me, Gabe?" I asked in a low voice. "That lady over there wants to talk to Ariana. Do you know if she's back?" Ariana had said she'd be in late today because of an appointment.

"I haven't seen her come in yet," Gabe said. "One sec, I'll talk to the customer." He finished ringing up and then came over to where the woman was standing. Her scowl was now a permanent part of her face.

"Can I help you, miss?" Gabe asked, giving a friendly smile.

The woman did not smile back. "Can you get me the fifty cupcakes I need? Because your coworker can't seem to grasp how urgent this is."

My mouth dropped. Was she calling me stupid? "That's not it," I said, my face getting hot. "You asked for the order to be ready today, and I didn't think that's possible. Right, Gabe?"

"That's usually right, but let me get the owner on the

phone," Gabe said. "One second. Do you want to have a seat and I'll get right back to you?"

The woman exhaled loudly. "Fine. But this better not take long. I have a hair appointment in thirty minutes."

Gabe picked up the phone behind the register. As he dialed Ariana's cell number, he mouthed to me, "Don't worry. I'll handle it."

I nodded, but inside I felt panicked. What if this woman complained to Ariana about me and I lost this job? I was trying to follow the bakery's policy, but what if that wasn't good enough? Ariana knew me well enough to know I would never try to offend someone on purpose—right? Suddenly I wasn't so sure.

This was her business, and I was still a kid. If she felt like I was messing things up for her and leaving a bad impression with her customers, she might have no choice but to fire me.

Thankfully nobody else was in line, so I took a second to go to the kitchen to get a drink of water. I took a few deep breaths to try to calm down. While back there, I watched as the kitchen crew worked on a separate custom cupcake order. It looked like it was for a baby shower, since they were cutting out fondant onesies and bottles to place on top of pastel-orange-and-teal swirled icing. I was much better at baking than customer service. I wished I could be in the kitchen helping them instead of dealing with mean customers.

Entitled. That was the word my mom would use for that woman. She thought that she deserved whatever she wanted, whenever she wanted it. She probably wasn't used to people saying "no" to her about anything.

At least most of the customers who came in here weren't like that.

But once again, I couldn't help but wish Marcus's restaurant would work out, that we could find a way to make it happen. Then I wouldn't have to work behind a register anymore and I could get back into the kitchen—my own professional kitchen.

I had to find a way to make this happen. Not in a few years, but now.

Chapter Sixteen

Maya asked me to help her get ready to meet up with Trevor, so on Saturday afternoon, Mom dropped me off at her house.

"Why aren't you hanging out with Maya and Hannah together?" Mom asked when we were in the car.

Hannah was coming over for the first time that night. Our plan was to bake something yummy, do facial masks, and then watch a movie.

"Maya has other plans." I was about to tell Mom that she and Trevor were going to hang out together, but then I remembered that Maya didn't want her parents to know they were more than friends.

But I *really* wanted to talk about it.

"Can you keep a secret?" I asked when we were at a red light.

Mom glanced at me through her sunglasses. "Of course. But if someone's in trouble, I can't promise to keep that to myself."

"It's nothing like that."

"Okay," Mom said. The light turned green, so she focused on driving again. "Then my lips are sealed. What's up?"

"Maya's plans . . . She's hanging out with Trevor tonight." I paused. "Just the two of them, in Davis Square."

"They're leaving you out?" Mom asked.

"No. I mean, they *like* each other now."

Mom quickly glanced at me again as my words set in. Her mouth formed a small smile. "They're going on a date?"

I laughed. "We don't call it that, but yeah."

"Wow. You kids really are growing up." Her face lit up, suddenly full of nostalgia. I knew that look. It was the same as when she told people stories from when I was little. "Patricia must be losing it. Her baby, going on his first date!"

I rolled my eyes. "I don't know if Trevor told her. And you can't say anything. It's a secret, remember? Maya said she didn't want to tell her parents yet. I think with every-thing going on with her dad, she doesn't want to deal with all their questions."

Mom nodded. "I understand." Then she said, "But you know you can talk to me, right? When you're ready to date? Or . . . hang out. Unless it's already happening . . . ?"

"No! I mean, it's not happening right now." I laughed nervously. "And I know I can talk to you."

Mom reached over and squeezed my knee. "Good."

We drove for a few more minutes. "I'm happy for Trevor and Maya, but I'm worried about what this means for our friendship," I said.

"I get that," Mom said. "Things may change now that they like each other, but I don't think how they feel about you as a friend will change. They both love you too much."

"Yeah. That's true." I smiled to myself, glad that I'd opened up to Mom and that she'd gotten it.

At Maya's house, she immediately started showing me outfits. She pulled out a couple of casual dresses from her closet.

"What are you guys going to do in Davis again?" I asked.

"First we're going to get crepes, and then we're going to watch a movie."

"Ooh, crepes. Fancy."

Maya giggled. "It was his idea. I feel like I should look nicer than normal. Should I wear a dress?"

"I guess. Let me see some options."

She held up a few different dresses. One was flowy with a flowery pattern, one was more formfitting in black-and-white plaid, and one was blush pink and had pockets.

"I love dresses with pockets," I said. "You should try the pink one."

"Good idea," Maya said as she took the dress to the bathroom that connected her room to her sister's room. "Then I have somewhere to put my hands if we don't hold hands right away."

I imagined the two of them walking through Davis Square at dusk, their hands clasped. I'd held Trevor's hand before, like when we were little and crossing the street with one of our parents. But not in a "I like you" way where your fingers interlock. Back then, Trevor's hands were sticky, and I let go as soon as I could.

I needed to change the subject. "How's your dad, by the way?" Maya's dad's surgery earlier that week had gone well. He'd spent a few days in the hospital but was home now.

"He's recovering," Maya said. "He's been sleeping a

lot, which my mom says is a good thing."

She came out of the bathroom in the pink dress, her hands in the pockets. She gave a little twirl.

"It's cute!" I said, which made her grin.

She looked herself over. "Okay, I'll wear this."

"Do you think Trevor is doing the same thing right now?" I asked. "Trying on different outfits and stuff?"

"I don't know. I can't believe this is happening. That I'm going out with Trevor, of all people."

"I can't either." I paused, and then said, "Do you think you'll . . . kiss?" As soon as the words came out of my mouth, I regretted asking. The mental picture of my two best friends kissing was way worse than them holding hands.

But if they were going to become a . . . thing . . . I'd have to get used to the idea.

Maya blushed. "I don't know!"

"Well, I hope you have a great time." I meant it, too. I really did want the two of them to be happy, even if it made me feel weird and left behind.

"Thank you," Maya said. "You're the best."

"But if Trevor does anything stupid, let me know," I added. "Don't think I won't kick his butt for you."

Chapter Seventeen

When Hannah's dad dropped her off at my house later that day, I brought her into the kitchen and showed her the ingredients I'd laid out: a bowl of egg whites, some cream of tartar, superfine sugar, gel food coloring, almond flour, and confectioners' sugar.

"Any guess what we're making?" I asked her.

"I have no idea . . ." she said after a few seconds of staring at everything.

"Macarons!"

"The coconut cookies?"

"No, those are macaroons. These are *macarons.*" I tried saying it with a French pronunciation, like I'd heard on baking shows. Macarons were delicate sandwich cookies with a chewy texture on the outside, and a filling—like a frosting or fruit puree—on the inside. Bakers usually dyed the shells pretty colors, so not only did the cookies taste delicious, but they looked beautiful, too.

I pulled up a picture on my phone and showed it to Hannah.

"Oh! I've tried those before, from a bakery in Boston. They're really yummy."

"They're not easy to make," I warned. "The ingredients have to be mixed perfectly. But I thought it could be a fun challenge." I'd watched a few tutorial videos the night before to prepare.

"I'm up for a challenge," Hannah said.

"Great." I handed Hannah an extra apron, which she put on.

"This feels so official," she said. "Like I'm in a baking class and you're my instructor."

I smiled. "Whenever I have money to spend, I usually buy baking stuff." I'd promised my parents that I'd keep half of my Ari's Cakes earnings in a savings account, but that still left plenty for more baking supplies.

I'd just gotten my second paycheck from Ariana the day before. Getting that check made the encounter with the awful customer the other day worth it. And thankfully,

Ariana hadn't fired me because of it; she hadn't said any-thing to me at all. I guessed she and Gabe had figured out the rush order.

"Before we get started . . ." I turned on my Bluetooth speaker and played the Little Tomato playlist. Earth, Wind & Fire's "September" started.

"What's this?" Hannah asked, bopping to the beat.

I filled her in on the Little Tomato playlist. "Since Marcus is out now and we don't have to write any more letters, I shared the playlist with him so he can add songs whenever he thinks of one."

"That's so nice that you've gotten close," Hannah said. I noticed some sadness in her voice.

"How are things with your mom?" I asked.

Hannah shrugged. "Fine, I guess. I haven't talked to her. She'll call and talk to my brother, but I don't really want to hear what she has to say."

"Oh."

"My dad wants me to start seeing a counselor. Like, a therapist. He's worried that I haven't taken Mom's calls in months. I have to go next week."

"Wow. Are you nervous?"

"A little. But Dad said I can talk about whatever I want, and the therapist won't judge me. So maybe it'll be good to talk all this out with someone."

I nodded. "I agree."

We spent the next thirty minutes baking. I'd done the first step—separating out egg whites—last night, since they had to sit in the fridge overnight. We added the cream of tartar to the egg whites and beat them until they looked like fluffy clouds. Then we added the sugar little by little until it all blended and got stiff.

"Watch this." I picked up the glass bowl and held it upside down. The mixture didn't move at all. I even shook the bowl a little.

"Wow, it's like magic," Hannah said.

"That's how we know it's ready for the next step. We can add the food coloring now. What's your favorite color?"

"An ocean blue. Kind of like my nails."

I glanced at her fingernails, which were painted a shimmery blue. "So pretty," I said.

"Thanks." Then she asked, "What's your favorite color?"

"Purple," I said.

"Can we mix them and make a purplish blue?"

"Okay!" We put a couple of drops of each color into the bowl and I slowly folded it in. It was important not to overmix.

Once the color looked right, we grabbed a second

bowl. We used a sifter to sift almond flour and confectioners' sugar into it. Then we slowly started mixing in some of the egg white mixture. Soon the batter looked shiny and smooth. We carefully poured it into a piping bag, and then piped circles of batter onto the baking sheet. I'd just bought a silicone mat that had small circles printed on it, to make this step easier.

"This is the fun part." I picked up the pan and banged it on the counter a couple of times "It's to get any air bubbles out of the batter. You try."

Hannah banged it too, and we laughed.

I used a toothpick to pop any other bubbles on the surface of the batter, a tip I'd seen on one of the videos I'd watched.

"Now we have to let it rest," I said.

"Let the batter rest?"

"Yeah. We can check on it in a half hour." I set a timer on my phone.

"These cookies really are high-maintenance," Hannah said. "Want to do the facial masks while we wait?"

"Sure! We can do them on the porch if you want."

"Okay."

We went outside and Hannah showed me the different masks she'd brought. A bunch of them had animal faces on the packaging. "You spend your money on baking stuff, and I spend mine on masks and nail polish."

I grabbed a mask with a panda face on it, and Hannah picked one that had a sloth. She showed me how to put mine on.

"We look ridiculous," I said, laughing. "Let's take a selfie."

We did, and then Hannah said, "Wait until you feel your skin when you take it off."

She was right. My face felt really smooth twenty minutes later when we took the masks off and went back inside to bake the macarons.

We put the cookies in the oven to bake, and I showed Hannah how to make the vanilla buttercream we'd use to fill them.

When the timer went off, I pulled the pan out of the oven and squealed. "They have feet!"

"They have *what?*" Hannah looked at me like I'd lost it.

I lifted the sheet so I could show her the ruffles that had formed at the bottom of each cookie shell. They weren't *perfect*, but they were there. "I don't know why they call them feet, but what I do know is that we achieved them, so yay!"

Hannah smiled. "Nice!"

We put the cookies together by piping some of the buttercream onto one shell and then adding another to the top. I arranged a few on a plate so I could take some pictures. They looked amazing!

When I picked up my phone, I saw a couple of texts from Maya. For the first time ever, a message from her made my stomach drop.

MAYA: it's going great! 😄

Then she attached a picture of her and Trevor, at a table with plates of dessert crepes in front of them. Maya was glowing, and Trevor looked super happy too.

I knew I'd said I'd wanted them to have a good time, but I couldn't help but feel . . . What *was* I feeling? Left out? Envious? Just not good.

I closed the message without responding, and opened the camera app. I took a few pictures of the macarons from different angles. "Let's taste them," I said to Hannah.

Hannah and I each grabbed one, and I took a bite. The cookie melted in my mouth.

"This. Is. Incredible," Hannah said. "I can't believe we baked these ourselves."

I beamed with pride. *Maybe I could make a special macaron flavor as a signature dessert in my restaurant with Marcus,* I thought. I took another bite, finishing the cookie.

"Let's take selfies with the cookies this time."

"Yes!" Hannah picked up the plate of macarons and held them up next to me.

I reached my arm out and captured our smiling faces plus the cookies. We took a couple of silly ones too, where we opened our mouths wide like we were about to attack the plate.

"Enough of that," Hannah said. "Let's eat some more."

I closed the camera on my phone and then turned it off completely, so no more texts could ruin this happy mood.

Chapter Eighteen

It was a beautiful day in Beacon Hill the next time Marcus and I were both working at Ari's Cakes. During our lunch break, we decided to eat our lunches quickly, and then finally check out one of the landmarks on the Black Heritage Trail.

The first stop on the trail map that we'd found online was the Robert Gould Shaw and Fifty-Fourth Regiment Memorial. It was on the corner of the Boston Common, Boston's biggest park. We walked down Joy Street, which was a narrower street lined with brick apartment buildings and brownstones. The sidewalks were also made of brick.

"Can you believe this was a free Black community once upon a time?" Marcus asked.

When Marcus and I grabbed lunch near the bakery or whenever I explored this neighborhood on my own, I usually only saw white people. "There doesn't seem to be a Black community here . . . anymore." I frowned.

"You're right about that," Marcus said. "I can't even imagine how expensive these brownstones must be now."

The self-guided tour website was open on my phone, so when we got to the memorial, I read the description. The Fifty-Fourth Regiment was the first Black regiment to be recruited to the North during the Civil War.

"Imagine having to literally fight for your own freedom," Marcus said, shaking his head.

Marcus knew what losing his freedom felt like. I couldn't even imagine.

We spent a few minutes staring at the monument and reading the inscriptions. Then, since we still had some time before we had to head back to work, Marcus and I sat down on a park bench.

"I have to talk to you about something," Marcus said, sounding more serious than usual.

"Is everything all right?" I asked.

"Yeah. I just wanted to let you know that this restaurant idea—we're going to have to put it on hold."

My eyebrows scrunched up. "Why? We barely got started with figuring it out."

"I know. But the more I think about it, the more I realize it's not realistic. I don't have enough experience for this. I worked in a kitchen for years, but it was a prison kitchen. Not a professional kitchen with customers who have high expectations."

"Well, you're working in a professional kitchen now, at Ari's Cakes."

"Right, but I only started," Marcus said. "And we're baking, not cooking."

I exhaled. "Maybe you don't believe you can do it, but I do. You're an amazing cook. My parents and Grandma all think so."

Marcus gave a small smile. "I appreciate that, Little T. I really do." He sighed. "The other thing is the finances. I reached out to a few other banks, and they all said the same thing as the first one. I need better credit and savings. I need to get my life back on track before I do something like this. If I do."

If? Now he was thinking of *never* trying to open a restaurant at all?

"Maybe it's not in the cards for me, and that's okay," Marcus continued. "It's a pipe dream. Something nice to think about when I was stuck in prison—besides being able to see you, of course. But I shouldn't have gotten you caught up in it. Things aren't perfect for me right now, but I'm getting back on my feet and I'm lucky. I don't need to distract myself with silly dreams right now. And you don't need to spend your time worrying about me. You should focus on your own life, okay? That's what I want most."

I didn't know how to respond. So I nodded instead. He sounded like he'd made up his mind. I was only fourteen years old. I couldn't open a restaurant right now without him.

"Well, if that's what you want . . ." I finally said.

"It is," Marcus said. "We can keep doing our Sunday dinners, cooking together. That would make me very happy."

"Okay."

It didn't feel okay. Not at all. But we had to head back to work.

Later that night, when I was trying to fall asleep, I thought about everything Marcus had said.

I knew this was Marcus's choice, but I had a feeling that if one of the banks had given him a loan, he wouldn't make the same decision.

He wasn't putting aside his dream because he was

happy with the way things were. It was because he didn't want to disappoint me.

He was giving up.

But this dream was mine too now. I'd always wanted to become a pastry chef. I figured when I grew up, I'd get a job working at a restaurant or in a bakery like Ari's Cakes. But to create a restaurant with Marcus? That would make it so much more special.

I wasn't ready to give up on this yet. And it wasn't fair for Marcus to have to, just because he'd spent time in prison. He shouldn't have to settle for less, not after all the ways he'd suffered while paying for a crime he never committed.

Now that I thought about it, he'd done something similar when I'd wanted to find his alibi witness. He told me to forget he mentioned it and focus on my own life. He had wanted to protect me back then, and he still wanted to protect me. Even if it meant sacrificing his own happiness.

I thought about the poetry segment that we'd done in eighth grade on the African American poet Langston Hughes. We read and discussed several of his poems. One was about all the bad things that could happen if you deferred a dream, and the other one was Hughes saying that you should always hold on to your dreams.

I loved them both because I loved to dream big. I even printed them out and put them on the bulletin board above my desk in my room.

Marcus deserved his dream, more than anyone else who I knew.

No way could I let him give up on it.

Chapter Nineteen

Before I brought up the restaurant to Marcus again, I needed to figure out how we could make it happen. If I had a solid plan, Marcus wouldn't be able to turn it down. If banks wouldn't give him a loan, and the state wouldn't give him the wrongful conviction compensation he deserved, there had to be another way to get the money we needed.

I texted Trevor to see if he was around, since he was good at helping me brainstorm. He didn't respond right away, which made me wonder if he was hanging out with Maya again or was too busy texting Maya to talk to me. We'd barely spent any time together that summer.

I went outside and knocked on his door. I waited a couple of minutes, but nobody answered. If this was any other summer, he'd be around. Us hanging out would be a given. Already, things were changing between us.

I slogged back up to my room. Guess I'd have to brainstorm on my own.

I got out a notebook so I could write down any ideas that came to me. But at first, all I could think of were more questions. Like, how many other exonerees struggled to get back on their feet after prison? There was that article that Marcus had sent me about other Massachusetts exonerees. Was it just as hard in other states?

I got on my computer and typed "exonerees" into Google. The first few results were definitions of the word, but then I saw a link from the Innocence Project's page. When I clicked through, I saw that it was about a yearly Innocence Network Conference that happens every spring, where exonerees could come together for support.

Wow. If there was an entire conference dedicated to this, it was clearly a big problem.

I also saw that there was a dedicated Wrongful Conviction Day every October. I clicked around and found pictures from past celebrations. I couldn't help but notice how many people of color were in those photos. It made sense, since when I'd first researched wrongful convictions a couple of summers ago, I found out that more innocent Black people are wrongfully convicted. It made sense that they'd also be the majority of the exonerees.

Maybe that's why nobody was doing anything about this. If the majority of exonerees were Black, then it shouldn't have surprised me that Massachusetts and other states were not going out of their way to make sure these people had the resources they needed once they got out. That wasn't how America was set up, and that wasn't necessarily going to change anytime soon. Which sucked.

I couldn't fix an entire broken system, but maybe there was something I could do to make people care more about how messed up this was. I couldn't change this for every exoneree, but maybe I could change it for Marcus.

I was still thinking about all of this when Grandma drove me to Ari's Cakes the next day.

"You're really quiet this morning," she said. "Is everything all right?"

"Yeah," I said. "I'm just bummed about a couple of things."

"Want to talk about it?" Grandma asked. "We can even do something together when I pick you up later. I miss my summer Zoe time."

"I do, too." I smiled at her. "I'd love that."

Knowing that Grandma and I had plans after work put me in a better mood for the rest of the day. I tried not to think about the restaurant stuff in the meantime. Maybe Grandma could help me figure out a plan.

"What should we do?" Grandma asked when I got in her car again after work.

I looked out the window. "It's still pretty nice out. Want to walk along the Charles?" The Charles River ran through Boston, and the part near Harvard Square was scenic and peaceful.

"Sure," Grandma said. "Let's grab some iced tea first."

We went to her favorite tea place, where I got iced passionfruit, and she got iced lemon mint. Then she drove us into Harvard Square and parked in one of the public lots.

"Every time I come to this area, I think about how you rode the T here on your own," Grandma said as we walked down the street, past restaurants and shops, toward the river. "You and Trevor." She shook her head at the memory of it.

"Don't remind me." That had been one of the most stressful days of my life. I still had zero regrets about our Great Harvard Adventure to find Professor Thomas, since if I hadn't done it, maybe Marcus would still be in prison. But I'd also never seen Grandma or my parents more disappointed in me. I didn't want to disappoint them ever again.

"Well, you've already grown and matured so much since then," Grandma said. "I'm so proud of how well you're doing with your first real job." She put her arm around my shoulder and hugged me to her as we walked.

I looped my arm around her waist. "Thanks, Grandma."

We reached the Charles River and walked until we found a bench in the grass next to the water. We sat down and I watched a team of rowers go by with their oars in their long, skinny boat. It was hot out, but there was a nice breeze.

"What were you feeling down about earlier today?" Grandma asked.

I shifted in my seat so I faced her. "You know how Marcus wanted to open a restaurant?"

Grandma nodded.

"He said I should forget about it. Since he can't get a loan from anyone, and doesn't have any other money, he wants to let that dream go. But I think he was only saying that to make me feel better about it not happening. Like if he made it seem like he didn't want to do it, I wouldn't feel bad either. But now I feel worse."

"I see."

"I wish there was more that I could do." I paused, and then asked, "Did you think it would be hard for Marcus when he got out of prison?"

"I knew he'd have some struggles," Grandma said. "Because even though he was innocent, he lived the life of a guilty man in that prison for over a decade. He was treated like a guilty man inside, and that history is following him now."

"What can I do to help him?" I asked.

"What you're already doing, baby. Just keep being supportive. Marcus is going to be fine. I promise. We've had some great conversations since he's lived with me." Grandma sipped her iced tea, and then said, "And I know he had that restaurant dream, but I'm pretty sure being out of prison and spending all this time with you is his biggest dream come true."

I smiled at that. Maybe Grandma was right, and I should let this go. Especially since Marcus had told me to himself. But deep down, I still really didn't want to.

I looked back out at the water, where two ducks had climbed out of the river not far from us.

"I had this whole idea to create a signature dessert if we opened the restaurant," I said. "I should probably forget about that now, too."

"Only if you want to," Grandma said. "But you love

baking, so why not keep brainstorming? I'll tell you what—a signature Zoe Washington dessert will always be welcome in my house."

We both smiled.

"Okay," I said. "I'll keep thinking of ideas." For signature desserts and how to open this restaurant. Because even after this conversation with Grandma, I still wasn't ready to give up.

Chapter Twenty

It seemed like if anything was going to change, more people needed to know about the struggles exonerees experience after prison. Not only that, but they needed to *care*. They needed to see the problem and want to do something about it.

It's what had made all the difference for Marcus. First, I learned that innocent people could really end up in prison. That made me want to find out the truth about Marcus. Then that started a whole chain of events that led to him finally being released.

But this was about more than one person. There were

so many exonerees with their own stories. I needed to raise awareness.

But how?

Maybe I could start a social media page. But how would I get people to follow me and pay attention? It'd be better if someone with a big platform talked about this. Like a celebrity. But I didn't know any celebrities. Maybe I could write to some and see if they would want to collaborate.

Right, I'm sure an email from a random fourteen-year-old would make a celebrity sit up and pay attention. I rolled my eyes at myself.

What else could I do?

And then it hit me. I knew someone with a platform *and* an audience.

John Gallagher at Boston Public Radio!

My interview with him had been enough to inspire Hannah to come visit me at Ari's Cakes. Hearing me talk about having a parent in prison had made her feel less alone.

I knew Marcus's story made a difference for a lot of people, too, since he'd gotten his own messages from listeners. One woman had emailed him to say she felt more optimistic about her brother's wrongful conviction case after hearing him speak.

There needed to be more interviews with exonerees. John Gallagher and Boston Public Radio could do that. They had the platform and the listeners to make a difference.

Maybe I could write an email to John and ask him to do more interviews like the one with Marcus. But instead of only talking about how they got out of prison, they could talk about what it was like now that they were out. I'd had no idea so many exonerees struggled. I was sure most other people didn't know either.

I grabbed my laptop and searched for John Gallagher's name. The first website listed was his page on the Boston Public Radio website. I didn't see an email address for him, but at the bottom of the site, I found a contact page for the radio station.

I clicked on that and found a form to fill out. It said that a staff person would respond within three days. Perfect!

I filled in the fields with my name and email address. In the dropdown menu next to "What can we help you with?" I selected "Programs and Schedule." Then in the dropdown next to the following field, "Tell us more," I selected "Feedback about a show."

In the description field, I wrote out my message.

Dear Boston Public Radio,

My name is Zoe Washington, and I was a guest on your show with John Gallagher. The segment was about Marcus Johnson, my birth dad, who was wrongfully imprisoned and recently released.

I'm writing with a suggestion. Would you consider interviewing more exonerees? This could make a great series on your station. I recently found out that a lot of exonerees have a tough time living a normal life after they get out of prison. They have to basically start their lives over from scratch. It's not exactly fair that they should struggle so much after spending years and years doing time for a crime they didn't even commit. I think more people should know about this issue so something can be done about it. Boston Public Radio would be a great place for these kinds of conversations.

Thank you for considering.

Sincerely,

Zoe Washington

There. I knew this was a really good idea. I hoped they'd agree to it.

I read my message over a few more times and clicked Send.

Now I just had to wait.

I could not stop checking my email over the next few days to see if someone at Boston Public Radio had replied to my message. Finally, at the end of my lunch break on Friday, there was a response. I immediately opened it.

> Dear Zoe,
> Thank you so much for reaching out to us. We remember your segment with John, and it was a fantastic interview. You were a natural.

I smiled at that and read on.

> We appreciate your suggestion. Unfortunately, we aren't going to be able to do a whole series on this issue at this time, though we do understand its importance.
> Thank you for your support of Boston Public Radio.
> Take care,
> Tyler

My heart sank all the way down to my toes. They'd rejected my idea.

If they knew how important this was, then why were they saying no?

After reading the message again, I shoved my phone into my backpack and returned to work.

My mind raced as I helped Gabe put more cupcakes into our display case at the front of the shop.

Boston Public Radio was part of the problem. If nobody was willing to talk about these issues in front of their large audiences, nothing would change. Maybe another radio station would be willing to take this on.

Or maybe . . . maybe I needed to take matters into my own hands and interview exonerees myself. What if I started a podcast? Dad listened to them all the time. I'd listened to a baking podcast called *The Sweetest Podcast*, which had interviews with professional pastry chefs. Ariana was interviewed for it once, which was how I found out about it.

I bet I could figure out how to create my own. All I needed was some recording equipment, and to learn how to upload the file to all the podcast sites. Then I could figure out how to reach listeners.

Marcus could help me find people to interview. I could even talk to one of his Innocence Project lawyers and then ask them to connect me with some of their other exonerated clients. The Innocence Project had a platform. Maybe they could help spread the word about my podcast, so more people would listen.

As soon as I got home from work, I went onto my computer and looked up "how to start a podcast." A bunch of articles popped up, and even some YouTube videos. For the next hour, I watched and absorbed and took a lot of notes.

I didn't even notice when Mom knocked on my doorframe and walked into my room.

"Dinner's ready," she said.

Without looking away from the computer screen, I said, "Be right there."

"What are you staring at?" Mom came closer to my desk and read what was on my computer screen. "You want to start a podcast?"

"Yes!" I filled her in on my idea. "Is that okay? I was looking up what I need to get started, and it's only two things. A microphone that can connect to my laptop and editing software. My laptop already has an audio editing program on it, and the microphone isn't too expensive. See?" I showed her my notebook where I'd written everything down.

Mom looked at it and then back at me. "You want to interview other exonerees?"

"Yeah. I can interview one of Marcus's lawyers first. They could help give an overview of the problem, since they must have a lot of clients who go through this. And then I'll see if they can connect me with other exonerees to talk to. You or Dad could come with me, or I could interview them on a video call."

"That's an interesting idea," Mom said.

"I was thinking I could talk to them about their struggles, but also the positive experiences. Like how Marcus's story was more of a happy ending. I feel like more people need to know what it's really like for exonerees and their families. That it isn't automatically easy once the person gets out of prison. Marcus has been lucky, but lots of people aren't."

"I know that's right," Mom said. "Well, let me think. I don't know how I feel about you putting yourself out there like that."

"Like what? You already let me do the Boston Public Radio interview. They have way more listeners than I'll probably have." I could only hope I could get that many listeners for my own podcast.

"True. But they were good about keeping your privacy. They didn't say your last name on air."

I gave her a look. "Mom. My new friend Hannah literally found me at Ari's Cakes after hearing me on the show."

"Because *you* told everyone you work there, which I wasn't thrilled about."

"I promise I won't share too much personal info on my podcast. Except for my full name. It won't sound legit if I just go by Zoe. And anyway, I'll be the interviewer. The focus will be on the exonerees whose stories need to be told. Please, can I do it?" I looked at Mom with pleading eyes. I even stuck my lower lip out like I used to do when I wanted something as a little kid.

Mom thought for a few long moments. "What if I did this with you? I could help you record or edit the files. Then I'd feel more comfortable."

"Deal!" I hugged her. "I'd love your help. Thank you!"

"You're welcome," she said as she squeezed me back. "Now let's go down and eat before the food gets cold."

After dinner, I ordered a USB microphone. The website I ordered from had free two-day delivery, so it would be here by Monday. I decided to use the rest of the weekend to plan the podcast, so I could start recording right away.

I went into the podcast app on my phone and downloaded some episodes of other popular interview shows. I noticed some of the newer podcasts had short teaser episodes, where they told listeners what they could expect once episodes dropped. I got my notebook back out and started writing a teaser script. I'd record it as soon as the microphone arrived.

When I finally went to bed, my brain was brimming with ideas and hope.

Chapter Twenty-One

Trevor and his mom, Patricia, came to our next Sunday dinner. Mom and Dad drove them over to Grandma's house when it was time to eat. I was excited to get to hang out with Trevor, since I hadn't seen much of him all week. I also hadn't seen much of Maya, because between my job, and her extended family visiting to see her dad, there hadn't been any time. I think whatever free time Trevor and Maya had, they spent together.

That night, Marcus made pork chops, macaroni and cheese, and green beans. For dessert, I made strawberry shortcake with homemade biscuits from scratch, fresh whipped cream, and strawberries I'd gotten from the farmers market. It was nice to get back into the kitchen after spending the weekend on my computer planning my podcast.

"How have things been for you, Marcus?" Patricia asked once everyone had started eating.

"Pretty good, actually," Marcus said. "I can't complain."

"That's great," Patricia said. "This food is outstanding. Trevor said you and Zoe might open up a restaurant?"

I'd forgotten that I hadn't told Trevor that Marcus wanted to put the idea on hold. He lived right next door, and he still had no idea what was going on with me.

"Oh, that's on the back burner for now," Marcus said.

Trevor looked at me and mouthed, "Really?"

I nodded.

"It's because it's too expensive," I said, not sure if I should mention Marcus's bank loan rejection.

"You should start a Kickstarter," Trevor said. "Isn't that what people use them for—to raise money for stuff like this?"

"What's a Kickstarter?" Marcus asked.

"A fundraising website," Dad chimed in.

"Yeah," Trevor said. "You tell people what you're raising money for, and they donate."

"That's not a bad idea," I said. See, this was why I wanted to brainstorm with him. I couldn't believe I hadn't thought of a Kickstarter myself. "We can reach out to all our family and friends. And anyone who messaged us after our radio interview. Maybe they'd donate to our restaurant fund, too." I got more excited with each word.

Marcus looked unsure. "We don't need people's hand-outs."

"It's not really like that," Trevor said. "People donate because they want to see the end result. Like, I donated twenty bucks to this game company, and now that they got their funding, they're going to be able to make the game, and then I get to play it. Without donors, that may not have happened. In your case, the donors will get to eat at your restaurant once it's open."

The more I thought about this, the more perfect it sounded. "I could plug the Kickstarter on my podcast!"

"Don't get ahead of yourself, Zoe," Mom said. "This is Marcus's decision."

"What podcast?" Trevor asked.

"What's a podcast?" Marcus asked.

I explained everything, including how I had reached out to Boston Public Radio, and they'd rejected the idea.

"That sounds really interesting, Zoe," Grandma said. "I can't wait to listen."

"Me too, once you show me how," Marcus said, laughing. "And I do know a couple of people you could interview."

"Great! So, you'll consider the Kickstarter?" I asked Marcus. "When we're finished with dinner, we can go look at the website and see what it's all about."

"It's so hard to say no to you," Marcus said.

I grinned. "So . . . don't . . ."

"Let's look at the website after dinner. I can at least agree to that."

"Wait, but aren't we having dessert?" Trevor asked. "I know it's not chocolate, but those biscuits look really good."

Everyone laughed.

"After dessert, then," Marcus said.

After we finished eating—dessert included—my parents and Patricia helped clear the table and do the dishes. Marcus, Trevor, and I huddled around Grandma's computer, where I typed in the address of the Kickstarter website. We looked around and found the guidelines for starting a new project.

Trevor pointed to the screen. "See, it says right there that it should be something you share with other people. A restaurant would do that."

We read through the rest of the rules, and it all seemed

straightforward. This could work for us. We could create a project, ask people to donate, and use that money to open our restaurant. No bank loan, credit history, or background checks needed. We just had to find people to contribute, but that was under our control.

"Marcus," I said, spinning around in Grandma's desk chair to face him. "I know you said you were fine with putting this restaurant aside, but I think, deep down, you still really want to do it. Right?"

Marcus didn't answer at first, only stared at the Kickstarter website some more.

"Will you let us do this?" I asked. "Please?"

Finally, Marcus looked at me, and there was a glimmer of hope in his eyes. It might've been a small glimmer, but it was there. "Let's see," he said. "This might not even work. We might not get enough people to donate."

"But then we'll be no worse off than we are now," I said. "If that happens, then we'll wait a few more years. But think about if we do get enough people to donate . . . We could actually start a restaurant together now."

It was clear from Marcus's face that this possibility made him happy. I knew he still cared about this.

"Okay. Sounds like we'd have to put some work into describing the project, to convince people to donate. I need to do some more research to see how much money we actually need."

"I bet Ariana could help us with that," I said. "She must've had to put something like that together to open her bakery. She should know the costs."

Marcus nodded. "It won't hurt to try. I'll talk to Ariana tomorrow."

"Yes!" I hugged Marcus tight, and he laughed. "This is going to work. I can feel it."

And then I hugged Trevor. "Thank you for that idea," I said.

When I let go, he was grinning. "No problem."

"Trevor, it's time to go," Patricia called out from the living room.

"You too, Zoe," Mom said.

"We're coming," I said.

I gave Marcus and Grandma goodbye hugs, and then the rest of us squeezed into Dad's car to head home.

"I'm so glad you came," I told Trevor when we got to our front porch. "But I wish we had longer to talk. Want to come over tomorrow after camp? You can help me set up my podcast stuff if you want."

"Okay," he said. "Yeah, I'll come by."

"Great. See you then."

We said goodbye and I headed up to my room, more optimistic than I'd felt in a while.

Between this podcast and the Kickstarter, my summer was about to get a lot busier.

Chapter Twenty-Two

I ran up our porch stairs as soon as I got home from work the next day. While I'd been at Ari's Cakes, I got an email saying my microphone had been delivered. There were a couple of packages by our front door, and one of them had my name on it. It was here! The last time I had been this excited about a piece of mail, I was secretly writing to Marcus.

I brought the box up to my room and ripped it open with a pair of scissors. The microphone wasn't fancy, but it was one of the recommended ones that I could afford with my Ari's Cakes money. The last couple of nights, I'd listened to a bunch of podcast episodes from different shows, to get a sense of what style I wanted mine to have. I'd also watched a ton of YouTube tutorials and read articles about how to record and edit a podcast.

I was ready.

All I needed now were people to interview. But I already had my first guest scheduled. During our lunch break today, Marcus had texted one of his Innocence Project lawyers to ask if I could interview her. She agreed, so Mom and I scheduled time to meet with her on a video call on Thursday.

In the meantime, to get some practice in, I decided to record a short promo episode to upload. I plugged the microphone into my laptop right as I heard a knock on my door.

It was Trevor.

"Oh hey. You're just in time."

"Hey." He came in and sat on my bed. "Sorry, I had to shower when I got back from camp."

"Please don't apologize for not showing up smelly." I laughed.

He looked at the microphone connected to my laptop. "Have you recorded anything yet?"

"Not yet. I'm about to."

"What's your podcast going to be called, anyway?" Trevor asked.

"I don't know yet," I said. "I need to think of something soon. Do you have any ideas? I want it to sound official. Like if someone was browsing through podcasts on their phone, and started listening to mine, they'd be surprised to find out a fourteen-year-old is the host."

Trevor nodded. "What's the name of the show you were on with Marcus?"

"Boston Public Radio's Interview Hour," I said. "It's kind of boring."

"How about, 'Zoe Washington's Interview Hour'?"

"Then it sounds like I'm ripping them off. Though I kind of like the idea of my name being in the title."

"Should the name also have something about how you're interviewing people who went to prison?"

I shook my head. "Probably not. Because maybe I'll want to talk about something else after I'm done with this series. Who knows? Maybe this'll become my new calling—after baking, of course."

Trevor picked up the microphone and spoke into it. "What about, 'On the Mic . . .'" He gave a dramatic pause, and then said, "'with Zoe Washington.' I feel like fancy news shows always have 'with so-and-so' at the end."

I nodded. "Yeah." I wasn't sure about "on the mic," but I liked "with Zoe Washington."

"What about . . ." I started, and then stopped, scrapping my initial idea. But then I had it. "'On Air with Zoe Washington!'"

Trevor repeated it to himself. "I like that."

"Me too. It's simple but sounds legit."

Trevor nodded.

"Now I need a logo." I showed Trevor some of the podcasts I'd downloaded onto my phone. Each show had its own square logo.

"I know what you can use." Trevor grabbed my laptop and started searching for something. "Here." He showed me the screen. "When my brother started his video game review website, he paid somebody to make a logo. He said it was cheap. This website has graphic designers who'll make all kinds of things. See, for a podcast logo it only costs like fifteen dollars."

"That's perfect!" I said. "Thanks, Trevor."

"No problem."

I bookmarked the page and then closed my laptop. Now that Trevor was here, I didn't want to spend all our time staring at my computer. I swiveled in my desk chair to face him.

"So, what's new with you?" I cleared my throat. "How are things . . . with Maya?"

Trevor grinned. "Really good. She came to one of my basketball games last week. The other guys on my team were making fun of me, 'cause I guess my whole demeanor changed when she showed up."

"That's great," I said, feeling a little jealous. Not about them being together, but about them hanging out together when I'd barely seen either of them.

Well, he was here now. I got up from my seat. "I can finish this podcast stuff later. Wanna watch a movie or something?"

"Sure."

"I think I have leftover chocolate chip cookie dough in the freezer, from the last time I made a batch."

Trevor's eyes lit up. "Yesss."

We headed downstairs to put some cookies in the oven to bake. We also convinced Dad to order Chinese food for dinner. (It didn't take that much convincing since crab rangoon is one of Dad's weaknesses, and our local Chinese place makes the best.)

"Can I get your opinion on something?" I asked Trevor after our stomachs were full and we were supposed to be watching the movie.

"Sure."

"I'm trying to think of another Zoe Washington

dessert. Like the Froot Loop cupcakes, but different. Something Marcus and I could serve in our restaurant."

Trevor laughed. "Hold up. Aren't you doing enough this summer? You've got your job, now a podcast, a Kickstarter maybe—and you want to invent a new dessert?"

I shrugged. "I can't help that I'm interested in a lot of things! Plus, baking helps me relax after doing that other stuff."

"Don't get me wrong," Trevor said. "I know you'll get it all done. It's just like, dang. Sometimes I feel like an underachiever next to you."

"Wait, really?"

"I mean, no. I'm mostly kidding. I think it's cool. You inspire me."

"Stop," I said with a laugh.

"No, for real." From the look on Trevor's face, I could tell he was being sincere.

I shoved him lightly. "You're going to make me cry."

"Don't cry. Okay, so a new Zoe Washington dessert. Tell me more."

I explained how Grandma had encouraged me to keep dreaming up ideas even if the restaurant doesn't work out. "But I'm not sure what to come up with that feels unique. If you were at a barbecue restaurant, what would you want to eat after your meal?"

Trevor gave me a look.

"Chocolate," we said in unison.

"Right," I said.

"I did try something the other day and thought that you could make a way better version," Trevor said.

"Really, what?"

"A whoopie pie. You know, like a sandwich cookie, but the cookie part is cakier?"

"Yeah, I know those."

"One of the guys at camp had a birthday, and his mom brought a box for our group to share. It was good—I mean, it *was* chocolate—but it could've been a lot better. I gave it a . . . four out of ten."

"Ooh, a challenge. Okay, I'll try baking those and see what I can come up with. I bet I can make them a ten out of ten." I paused. "Thanks, *Trev*." I said "Trev" the way I remembered Maya saying it during our movie night.

Trevor gave a shy smile and shook his head.

"It's a cute nickname," I teased. "Maybe I should start calling you that, too."

Now he was the one to lightly shove me, but then we both laughed.

It felt good to laugh with Trevor. But it was bittersweet. I had no idea when we'd get to hang out like this again.

* * *

The next morning, I woke up early and went over my teaser episode script. I made a few changes, including adding my podcast title. Then I opened the audio recording program on my laptop and clicked Record.

Transcript Excerpt from
***On Air with Zoe Washington* Teaser Episode**
Published on Tuesday, July 26

Zoe: Hi! I'm Zoe, and you are listening to *On Air with Zoe Washington*, a brand-new interview podcast series. Our first season will be all about life after incarceration when you've been wrongfully convicted. If you're thinking, "What does 'wrongfully convicted' even mean?" keep listening. I'll tell you what you need to know and why this is so important.

In upcoming episodes, I'm going to interview lawyers, exonerees, and family members about how hard it is to get back to a normal life after prison. The struggles these innocent people experience may surprise you.

I bet you're wondering: Why is a fourteen-year-old girl starting a podcast about *this* topic? Well, it's personal to me. Let me give you a little of my background. It all started two years ago, on my twelfth birthday. I received a letter. . . .

Chapter Twenty-Three

Now that my podcast was underway, Marcus and I had to set up our Kickstarter project so we could start spreading the word and finding people to help fund it.

Marcus and I decided to meet at the library after work on Tuesday. He took the bus from his nonprofit job, and Dad dropped me off after picking me up from Ari's Cakes.

"How about when you're done here, we finally get some J.P. Licks?" Dad asked when he pulled in front of the library.

I smiled. "Deal."

Marcus was inside looking at a book display near

the checkout counter. "Hey, Little T," he said when he saw me.

"Hey, Big T." I shifted my backpack, which had my laptop inside. "Let's go find a table."

I led him upstairs to the adult nonfiction section. "You know," I said in a low voice, "when you were writing to me from prison and first told me you were innocent, I came here to look up books about wrongful convictions."

"Really?"

"Yeah."

We found an empty table and I pulled out my laptop.

"I talked to Ariana about the costs of starting a restaurant," Marcus said. "So we can figure out how much money we need to raise."

"And?"

"It's a lot, Zoe," Marcus said. "I knew it'd be a lot, but it's much more than I expected."

"Okay . . . that's fine. I'm sure we can get enough funders if we try."

"Ariana actually made a really good suggestion," Marcus said. "What if, instead of raising money for a whole restaurant, we raise money for a food truck instead?"

I frowned. "But I thought your dream was to own your own restaurant."

"True, but these things sometimes happen in stages. Did you know Ari's Cakes started out as a food truck?"

"I totally forgot about that." It had been years ago, when I was a lot younger. Ariana first started selling cupcakes from her home kitchen, and then she got a food truck. She even brought the truck to our driveway and served cupcakes at my fourth birthday party. I didn't really remember much about that party anymore, but I did remember getting to go inside the truck, and thinking Ariana was the coolest person ever. The truck even had the same branding as the bakery now.

"She said it was a great way to get started," Marcus said. "Because you don't have as many up-front costs. You can lease the food truck, which is a lot cheaper in the long run than renting restaurant space, furnishing it, and all that. We could still serve a nice menu this way and find different places around Boston to park. Then, if it goes well and we knew we'd have enough customers in the area, we could open an actual restaurant down the line."

"But, like, can you cook and bake in a food truck? Or only serve food?"

"Good question," Marcus said. "I asked Ariana the same thing. She said you can cook on the trucks, since there are stovetops. But there usually aren't any ovens. Ariana paid a professional kitchen to be able to bake there. She said if we did this, we could use her kitchen after hours. Depending on what kinds of desserts you wanted to serve, since it wouldn't be as big of a quantity, you could even bake at home."

I got quiet as I let all of this sink in. For the past few weeks, ever since Marcus first told me about his goal to open a restaurant, I'd been picturing us working together in a big, professional kitchen. We could pick out all the restaurant decorations. I could put together a whole dessert menu.

"We can take time to think about it," Marcus said.

"Well, it seems like we should decide for sure, because we have to write out our plans for the Kickstarter project," I said.

"In that case, I think we should start with the food truck. It'll be less up-front costs, so our Kickstarter goal won't have to be as big. That means there's a higher chance we'll get all the funding we need."

I nodded.

"And after talking to Ariana, I realized I'd feel more comfortable starting smaller anyway. I don't know anything about running a restaurant, but I'm pretty sure I can cook and sell off a truck. And we'll still get to work together."

"All right," I said. "You convinced me." I opened the

Kickstarter website on my laptop and clicked on the Start a Project button. "Let's get to work."

We didn't finish our whole Kickstarter page, but we made some progress. We were able to save what we had completed so far, so we made plans to get back to it the next day. One big thing we realized we needed was a name for our business. This was the second name I needed to brainstorm that week, and it was only Tuesday!

After all that hard work thinking and planning, I was ready for some ice cream. Marcus and I walked out of the library and saw Dad parked right outside.

"Hey, Paul," Marcus said when Dad rolled down the passenger side window.

"Hey. Did you two get a lot accomplished?"

Marcus nodded. "Some, yeah."

There was an awkward silence while I got into the car and buckled my seat belt. From the passenger seat, I looked at Dad and Marcus and wondered if they could ever be friends. Or if I'd always be the only thing they had in common. It would be so great for them to get to know each other better.

"All right, well, I'll see you later, Little T," Marcus said.

Without thinking, I blurted, "Do you want to come to J.P. Licks with us?"

Marcus looked surprised and when I glanced at Dad, he looked confused.

"Sorry, I don't know why I asked that. I just thought . . ." I shook my head. "Never mind."

I'd made things even more awkward. What had I been thinking? I knew this was supposed to be quality time with Dad. I wished I could go back thirty seconds and keep my mouth shut.

"It's all good," Marcus said. "I should head home anyway. Enjoy your ice cream."

"Right. Bye." I sank down in my seat.

Dad waved at Marcus and rolled the window back up.

We listened to the radio as Dad drove us to J.P. Licks. We were also quiet while he parked, and while we walked to the shop. There was a longer than usual line inside, probably because of the hot and humid weather.

Dad got two scoops of the red velvet cake ice cream, and I got two scoops of their salted caramel cookies 'n' cream flavor.

When we got outside with our cups, a couple was getting up from a bench, so I skipped over to grab the free seats.

"Sorry about earlier," I said. "I didn't mean to invite Marcus."

"It's okay, I get it," Dad said.

"And I'm sorry I've been so busy lately."

"It's all right, kiddo."

"Are you sure it's all right? You seem down or something."

"How could I be down while eating my favorite ice cream?" He took a huge bite, but then his face scrunched up. "Bad idea. Brain freeze."

I laughed.

"Can I taste yours?" I asked. "I haven't had red velvet cake mixed in with ice cream before."

Dad reached his cup over to me so I could take a spoonful. My eyes lit up as soon as I tasted it. "This is amazing," I said. The pieces of moist red velvet cake were mixed into the vanilla ice cream, but there were also swirls of cream cheese frosting. "Wow."

"Here." Dad handed me his cup.

"What? No. That's yours."

"We can switch. Since you like this so much."

Offering to give me his ice cream was so like him. It made me feel even guiltier about inviting Marcus along.

"Are you sure?" I didn't wait for him to answer. "Actually, let's share instead."

I took a scoop of the red velvet cake ice cream and put it in my cup. Then I took some of my salted caramel cookies 'n' cream and added it to his cup. Now we each had some of both.

"Good idea." He smiled.

"What should we do next?" I asked after I devoured the rest of the ice cream.

"Well, we just had something sweet for dinner, so how about some burgers for dessert?" He pointed to a popular burger place at the corner. "Want to see if we can get a table?"

I grinned. "Sounds like a plan."

Chapter Twenty-Four

I was watching a show in the living room the next night when my phone buzzed. Hannah's name appeared on the screen. It was a video call, so I walked upstairs to my room as I answered. "Hey, Hannah."

"Hey."

I closed my bedroom door behind me and lay on my bed. "Where are you?" I asked once I realized that whatever she was sitting on was moving.

"Oh. It's our swing." She got up from it and turned the phone around so she could show me a swing that hung from a tree. It was shaped like half an egg, and there was a cushion inside. I could see the back of a house behind it, so I guessed she was in her backyard.

"Nice. What's new?"

"Remember I told you that my dad is making me see a therapist?" Hannah asked. "I've seen her twice now."

"Oh yeah. How's it been?" I asked.

"Not bad, actually. The therapist's name is Miranda. She's nice."

"Really? That's great."

"Yeah. I can finally talk about everything I'm feeling about my mom without holding back. During the first session, I was shy and nervous, so I mostly just answered Miranda's questions. But the second time I felt more comfortable, and I ended up . . . vomiting up all my feelings about everything. When I left, I did feel a little better."

"Thanks for that mental image."

Hannah giggled. "It's true! I also liked that she didn't judge me for not wanting to talk to my own mom." Hannah paused and then said, "Actually, I decided to do something."

"What?"

"I'm going to write my mom a letter."

"Oh wow," I said. "But I thought you didn't want to talk to her."

"Well, Miranda asked if I thought about telling my mom some of the things I was venting about. Like, maybe

I'd feel even better if I told my mom instead of ignoring her calls. I'm not ready to talk to her on the phone or visit her in person yet. But I can write a letter. I can take my time and figure out exactly what I want to say."

"It does sound like it'll be easier to share your feelings that way," I said. "I loved writing letters to Marcus."

"What kinds of things did you talk about in them?" Hannah asked.

I glanced at my bookshelf, at the photo box where I kept all of Marcus's letters. "At first we were just trying to get to know each other." I remembered how excited I used to get every time a new letter arrived. How happy reading Marcus's words, in his neat handwriting, made me feel. How excited I was to immediately listen to whatever new (to me) song he'd recommended. Somehow, we'd formed a bond by writing to each other. It almost made me miss those days, even though it was way better now that Marcus was out of prison.

"Eventually we started talking on the phone more and more, and sent fewer letters," I added. "But we still sent them sometimes."

"I'm kind of nervous," Hannah admitted. "Like, how do I put all of these feelings into words? How much she's let me down? Let our whole family down."

"You can write that," I said. "It doesn't have to be

perfect. Just, like . . . vomit it all out to her."

Hannah flashed a small smile. "I don't want to get my hopes up that anything will change after I send it. But Miranda said this is more for me, anyway. That even if my mom doesn't respond how I want, I can feel better knowing I finally told her how I feel."

I nodded. I really hoped this worked out for her.

"What's your best-case scenario?" I asked her. "We should think positively."

Hannah thought for a second. "I want my mom to read what I write, understand my perspective, and then finally get her life together. I know it won't be easy, because she has an addiction. But I want her to try harder. Get a regular job, and her own apartment somewhere nice. I want her to put me and my brother before everything else."

"I hope that happens," I said. "When do you think you'll start writing the letter?"

"Tonight. I'll probably try to mail it out before this weekend."

"Good luck," I said. "Let me know when you send it."

"I will."

"So, what else is going on?" I asked.

"Let me show you this new nail polish color I got. It's so pretty." Hannah brought her phone up to her room and showed me the polish. It was a white with multicolored sparkles inside that reminded me of sprinkles. Then she showed me the rest of her polish collection. I made her promise to do my nails the next time we hung out.

That night, my mind wandered back to our conversation. I felt bad that her mom wasn't there for her. I hoped she took Hannah's letter seriously and made a change.

One thing Hannah had said stuck out to me: how she wanted her mom to get a regular job and an apartment. Wouldn't that be hard for her, with a criminal record? It seemed like it'd be even harder for her than for exonerees like Marcus since she was guilty of her crime. It sounded like this was not her first time in prison, either. If she wanted to build a better life, I wondered—could she even do it on her own?

I hoped for Hannah's sake that she could.

Chapter Twenty-Five

By the time Sunday rolled around again, and Marcus and I were getting groceries for dinner, we'd finished our Kickstarter project and were ready to publish it. We decided it'd be fun to have it go live once we were with the rest of our family.

There was only one more piece of information that needed to be filled in—a name for our food truck. We still hadn't settled on anything.

"What if we call it something with Tomato in the name?" I suggested. We were in the produce aisle picking out stalks of asparagus and one fresh pineapple. "Since I'm Little T and you're Big T."

"That could work," Marcus said as he dropped some asparagus into our cart. "I just worry that people might think we're serving Italian food. You know?"

"True," I said, a little disappointed. It would've been such a nice full-circle moment to have something with Little and Big Tomato on the side of our food truck.

"When you were dreaming up restaurant ideas in prison, did you ever think of any names?" I asked.

"Not really. I kept calling it 'my restaurant' or 'my place' whenever I thought about it. I'm not that great at naming things." He laughed to himself. "It's a good thing your mom named you. You may have ended up as Wakanda or something."

I laughed. "Like from *Black Panther?*"

He shrugged. "It was my favorite comic book as a kid."

We pushed the cart over to the meat aisle, where Marcus looked at the different cuts of beef.

Just then, a new song started over the supermarket speakers. I recognized the opening melody right away.

I nudged Marcus. "Do you hear that? It's our song!"

"Isn't She Lovely" by Stevie Wonder was the very first song from the Little Tomato playlist I'd created when Marcus and I first started exchanging letters.

"It's still one of my favorites." He hummed along as he

picked up some steaks and dropped them into our cart.

Then he stopped moving and turned to face me. "I have an idea. What if we pick something that ties into the music from our playlist?"

"Like what?" I asked.

Marcus stared into space as he thought for a second, but then said, "I don't even know. Naming things really is not my strength." He chuckled.

"We'll think of something. Worst case, we can ask Grandma and my parents for ideas during dinner."

I really wanted to come up with the name myself, so I kept brainstorming as we continued through the store. We needed a name by tonight so we could post our Kickstarter and start getting donors.

"Maybe it doesn't have to be that complicated," I said when we'd gotten all the rest of the ingredients we needed and were walking to the self-checkout aisle. "We're going to serve barbecue, right? So maybe 'BBQ' can be in the name."

"Makes sense."

Then it hit me. Maybe it'd be strange to have "Tomato" in the name since there aren't a lot of tomatoes in barbecue cuisine. But we could still tie in our nicknames in a different way.

"How about . . . 'Big and Little BBQ'? Big and Little refer to us, and BBQ tells people the kind of food we're serving."

Marcus nodded slowly. "I like that."

"Yeah?"

"I do. A lot, actually. It's simple, but still feels personal and represents us." He swiped his hand across the air like he was reading off a sign. "Big and Little BBQ Truck, coming soon."

I grinned. "It sounds great!"

He put his arm around me and hugged me close.

I was so excited about our Kickstarter page going live that I decided to make something celebratory for that night's dessert: pineapple upside-down cake with a gooey brown sugar topping. I used fresh pineapple instead of canned, so it wouldn't taste too artificially sweet.

When we'd finished eating the meal Marcus had cooked for us—steak, grilled asparagus, and mashed sweet potatoes, I carried the cake out on Grandma's cake stand. Marcus followed behind me with my laptop.

He placed it on the table next to the cake, so everyone could see the screen. It was open to our Kickstarter project.

"We wanted you all to be here when it goes live," I

explained. "After this, people can start donating."

"It looks great," Mom said as she stared at the screen. "I love that picture of you two."

At the top of the page was a photo of Marcus and I standing next to each other, with his arm around my shoulders. We were both wearing jeans, white shirts, and black aprons. Grandma had taken it for us.

Right after we got home from the grocery store, Marcus and I had added our business name to the Kickstarter project and read through it one last time. We had everything we needed: a $30,000 goal, a deadline, details about how we planned to use the money, and even some of our backstory. I included a link to our Boston Public Radio interview because I thought more people would donate if they knew more about who we were, what we'd gone through, and why this food truck was so important to us.

I scrolled down to where we could submit our project.

"Should we count down?" Grandma asked. Before anyone could answer, she said, "Ten, nine, eight . . ."

By "seven," my parents and Marcus had joined in.

My heart was racing fast by the time we got to "three, two, one."

I clicked Submit and we all cheered.

We'd done it. We'd created our Kickstarter! Next, we'd have to send the link to everyone we knew. "Send them all the link to my podcast, too!" I said. "The first episode goes up tomorrow."

I'd interviewed an Innocence Project lawyer, Claire Powell, a few days earlier on a video call. Thank goodness Mom had been there to help. Having her next to me made me feel less nervous, and she'd also helped me make a list of questions to ask.

Recording had gone well, but then we had to edit down the audio file, to cut out parts where I messed up what I wanted to say and needed to start over. Mom and I did it together, and I was proud of how it came out. We even added some music to my intro.

"How about some cake?" Marcus said.

"I can help serve," Dad said as he reached for the cake knife.

"How can I contribute?" Grandma asked, squinting at my laptop screen. "I want to be the first."

"Mom," Mom said to her. "No. If anyone is going to be first, it's me."

Grandma looked offended. "Excuse me?"

I smiled. "How about I text both of you the link, and you can race to see who goes first?"

While Dad passed around plates of cake, I copied our Kickstarter URL into a text to Grandma and both of my parents.

As soon as I did that, Mom and Grandma took to their phones.

A couple of minutes later, I refreshed our Kickstarter page. "We have our first donor, and it's . . . Grandma!"

She winked at me. "I've still got it."

I clicked through to see how much Grandma had donated: $1,000. My jaw dropped. "Grandma! Oh my gosh, thank you. Are you sure that's okay?"

"It's more than okay, baby," she said. "I am so proud of you both and I can't wait to be your first customer in line."

"Thank you," Marcus said, giving Grandma a hug.

Mom and Dad also donated, and it was incredible to see the tracker line at the top already filling in.

We ate cake and everyone promised to spread the word about the Kickstarter to everyone they knew.

The Big and Little BBQ Truck was on its way.

Claire: I'll never forget my first case with the
Innocence Project. A woman—I'll call her Amy—
was wrongfully convicted of arson and murder. By
the time we took her case, she'd been in prison for
eleven difficult years.

Zoe: Can you tell us what happened?

Claire: There was a bad house fire. Amy escaped in
time, but her husband, who'd been asleep upstairs,
passed away. Later, the fire marshal concluded
that the fire had been deliberately set. That's called
arson. Then the investigators found evidence: an
empty gas can in the garage, which was connected
to the kitchen, where they alleged the fire had been
set. They also determined a motive: Amy and her
husband were going through hard times and her

husband had an insurance policy that Amy would be able to access if he died. The prosecution was able to easily get a guilty verdict.

Zoe: But Amy wasn't guilty?

Claire: No. She said all along that the fire was an accident, and it was. When we got our hands on this case, we dug into the evidence and found errors on the original report that claimed the fire had been arson. That document was the main piece of evidence for her conviction, so once we proved it was inaccurate, we got her conviction overturned.

Zoe: She must've been so relieved to finally be free.

How's she doing now?

Claire: She's doing well. It's been several years since she was exonerated, but we keep in touch.

Zoe: Is this why you like working at the Innocence Project? To help people like Amy?

Claire: Yes. There are so many reasons why people

are wrongfully convicted. There are eyewitness error, false or inconclusive forensic evidence, false confessions, and inadequate counsel, to name a few. All of these reasons are why innocent people have their lives taken away.

I want to be part of the reason they get their lives back.

Chapter Twenty-Six

The countdown was on—and so was the pressure. Now that our Kickstarter was live, I had to do whatever it took to get it funded. I was the one who'd convinced Marcus to do this. It needed to succeed.

The thing about Kickstarter was that it was all or nothing. If we didn't raise the entire $30,000 goal in the next thirty days, none of our funders would be charged, and we wouldn't get a single cent. Now I was glad we'd switched to a food truck. Our goal amount was already a lot, but only a fraction of the cost of an entire restaurant.

I texted Trevor, Maya, and Hannah with the Kickstarter link, and I posted about it on social media. My parents said they'd email everyone in our family, as well as their friends.

On Monday morning, I woke up early so I could bake cookies for my parents to bring into work. They were going to tell their coworkers about the Kickstarter, so I thought sweet treats could help convince them to contribute.

When Marcus and I got to Ari's Cakes for our shifts, we told everyone about the Kickstarter, with Ariana's permission.

"It's bittersweet because if this happens, I'll lose two great employees," Ariana said to us. "But we'll all gain an incredible new food truck in town. So, it's worth it." She winked at me.

By the following weekend, we'd raised $6,000, 20 percent of our goal. That was a lot of money already. I couldn't believe how fast it was happening! I shared the good news with Trevor and Maya but decided to text them separately instead of in our group chat.

Maya responded first.

MAYA: That's amazing! Congrats! My parents donated. Since my other family is still here visiting, I sent them the link to donate too.

ME: Thanks!

ME: How are things? I miss you!

MAYA: I miss you too. Sorry I've been so busy with family

ME: It's ok I understand

MAYA: I don't have to do anything with them tonight. Are you free?

ME: Yeah! What should we do?

MAYA: Come bowling with us!

Us? Oh. I got it.

ME: You and Trevor?

MAYA: Yeah, but it won't just be the two of us. He's inviting his other friends too.

When had they made these plans? If I hadn't texted Maya first, when was she going to invite me? *Would* she have invited me?

Maybe I was being paranoid. Bowling sounded fun, and it would be nice to hang out with both Maya and Trevor again. If his other friends were around, then I wouldn't be a third wheel. I could even invite Hannah.

ME: Ok!

MAYA: Yay can't wait!

Dad dropped me off at the bowling alley. I would've carpooled with Trevor, but he said he was going to hang out with his basketball friends right before, so he'd see me there.

Inside, I rented my bowling shoes and found Maya. She was sitting in one of the seats in our lane area, sharing a plate of curly fries with Trevor.

Nobody else was with them. *Where are Trevor's friends?*

I walked up and said hi.

"Zo! Hey!" Maya stood to give me a hug, and from behind her, Trevor waved at me.

"Where's everybody?" I sat down across from them, on the seat next to the scoreboard. Had the plans changed? I'd asked Hannah to come tonight, but she was busy. Now I was starting to regret coming myself.

"They're renting their shoes and getting food," Trevor said.

Phew. "Great," I said.

"Want a fry?" Maya asked.

"Sure." I ate one and the salty goodness helped me relax.

A minute later, three boys came over with trays of food—chicken wings, mozzarella sticks, onion rings, and more fries. They also each had a large soda.

Trevor introduced them to me. I recognized one of the

kids from our school and found out that the other two went to different schools.

Then we started bowling.

I was having fun, but I noticed that whenever it wasn't Maya's turn, she was hanging on to Trevor like a sloth to a tree. We barely got to talk because she was always whispering something to him or laughing at whatever the other kids were talking about.

I wasn't the third wheel in this group, but I still felt . . . left out somehow.

When it was my turn again, I bowled a strike. "Yes!" I said, doing a little dance. But when I turned around, Maya and Trevor weren't even paying attention. Nobody was. Instead of saying anything, I went to the snack bar and got a soda.

Finally, our game was done. I got second place, after one of Trevor's friends.

I was about to text Dad to pick me up when I heard one of the other kids ask if anyone wanted to play laser tag. There was an arcade, plus laser tag, on the other side of the bowling alley.

"Yeah!" Trevor said. Then he turned to Maya. "M, you wanna come?"

What, was I invisible? Why was he only asking Maya?

"No, I'll stay here with Zoe," she said.

"Oh, I was going to head home," I said.

"No! Stay. We barely got to talk."

Whose fault was that? I wanted to say but didn't.

"Okay," I said.

We ended up all walking to the arcade side. While the boys went to play laser tag, Maya and I found seats next to a vending machine.

"Guess what I decided to do when we get to high school?" Maya asked.

"What?"

"I'm going to try out for the cheerleading squad." She grinned.

"Really?"

"Yeah. Since Trevor's going to be on the basketball team—I mean, he's trying out, and I'm sure he'll make the team. It would be fun if I was a cheerleader. Then I could cheer at his games."

I nodded. "That sounds fun."

Maya looked at me. "What? Do you not think I'd make the team?"

"No! I'm sure you will."

"Then what is it?"

I shouldn't have been surprised that once Maya finally started paying attention to me, she'd sense that something was wrong.

"I guess . . ." I started, and then stopped, not sure how to phrase it. "I'm happy that you and Trevor are happy. I just feel like he's getting between us, somehow."

"What do you mean?" Maya asked. "He literally brought his friends here. We're all hanging out together."

"Yeah, but this is the first time all night that the two of us have been able to have a conversation," I said. "And that's only because the guys went to go play laser tag."

"I wanted to spend time with my boyfriend," Maya said, sounding defensive. "It's normal."

I blinked. *Boyfriend?*

"Oh, so you two are . . . official . . . now?" I asked.

Maya couldn't help but smile a little. "Yeah. I finally told my parents about it too. He came over for dinner one night."

"Wow." I couldn't believe she hadn't told me. "See, this is what I'm talking about. Why didn't you tell me that when it happened?"

Maya exhaled. "Honestly, it seemed to me like you didn't want to know. I texted you the night we first hung out, sent you a picture of us, and you didn't even respond."

"What?" And then I remembered. That was the night I was baking macarons with Hannah. I'd turned my phone off after reading the text.

"The next time you texted, it was about something else." Maya shrugged. "You can't blame me for not sending you other updates."

"Is this how it's going to be?" I asked. "Now that you're officially going out, everything's always going to be about you two?"

"What? No," Maya said. "It's just, why can't you be happy for me? I have my first boyfriend and I feel like I can't talk to you about it."

"I *am* happy for you," I said.

"You're not acting like it."

Ugh! How can she say that? Maya wasn't understanding me. At all. I suddenly wanted to stand up and leave. But I knew that'd only make everything worse.

I leaned back in my seat, took a deep breath, and thought about what to say next. Meanwhile, Maya stayed quiet.

"I'm sorry," I finally said, keeping my eyes trained on my hands. "It's just different, since it's you and Trevor. We used to be a trio, you know? And I feel . . ." I stopped, not sure if I wanted to say it.

"What?" Maya asked.

I looked up at her. "I guess I feel like I'm being left behind."

As the words came out, I suddenly thought about Dad, and the little time we'd spent together ever since Marcus got out of prison. The two situations weren't the same, but I could understand how Dad could both be happy *and* sad about me spending so much time with Marcus. I felt both happy and sad about Maya and Trevor being together.

Maybe it was that realization, or that conversation, or the stress that had built up around the Kickstarter and my podcast, but suddenly, I felt like crying. My eyes welled up with tears.

"Oh my gosh, Zo," Maya said, immediately wrapping me into a hug. "You are not being left behind. Not at all." She sniffled, and I knew she'd started crying too. She always cried easily, especially when someone else cried.

I squeezed her tight. "You and Trevor are really cute together. I'm not just saying that because you're my best friends."

"Thanks," Maya said, squeezing me back.

"Uh, what's going on?"

We separated and saw Trevor standing across from us. He looked worried. "Is it your dad?" he asked Maya.

"No!" Maya said, wiping her eyes. "No, he's fine.

It's . . . Don't worry about it. We're good. Ignore us."

There was confusion all over Trevor's face. When Maya and I looked at each other, we burst into laughter. It made my eyes tear up again, but this time it felt like a release.

It was exactly what I needed.

Chapter Twenty-Seven

Maya messaged me as soon as she got home from bowling, and we ended up texting back and forth for a long time—until Mom made me put my phone away to go to bed. It felt like old times, and my heart swelled with happiness.

It made me want to fix things with Dad. I knew he wasn't mad at me, but I still felt guilty about inviting Marcus to our ice cream outing. I also felt bad about spending so much more time with Marcus lately. I wanted to make it up to Dad somehow.

On Sunday morning, I woke up with an idea. I sent a text, and as soon as I saw the response, I went downstairs to find Dad. He was in the living room, reading with a mug of coffee beside him. Coffee that I bet had gotten cold since he usually got so into whatever he was reading that he'd forget about his drink.

He wasn't too distracted by his book to notice me, though.

"Morning, kiddo," he said when I sat on the couch next to him. "Are you heading out with Marcus soon?"

"About that," I said. "Can you go to the grocery store with me, and then help me bake tonight's dessert?"

He looked confused. "I can . . . but don't you do all that with Marcus?"

"Technically," I said. "We're both in Grandma's kitchen when I'm baking, but he's usually focused on cooking dinner. I told him I was going to bake at home today, and he's fine with it. When it's time for dinner, we can drive to Grandma's together, with Mom."

"Are you sure?" Dad asked.

I nodded. "Yup. I thought it'd be nice to bake with you this time."

That made Dad smile. "Okay." He put his book down on the coffee table. "What's on tonight's dessert menu, Chef Zoe?"

"Chocolate whoopie pies with fresh whipped marshmallow filling."

"Mmm. That sounds great."

On the way to the grocery store, I explained how Trevor had challenged me to make a better whoopie pie recipe than the one he'd tried at basketball camp.

Dad laughed. "Does anyone love a food more than that boy loves chocolate?"

"I doubt it."

When we got back home with all our ingredients, we put on aprons and got to work. Whoopie pies seemed simple to make, but what I'd learned about baking was that even if there weren't a lot of steps in a recipe, how you completed those steps mattered. If your ingredients were too cold, or you overmixed your batter, or you didn't get the baking time right, it could lead to disaster.

I wanted these to be the best whoopie pies Trevor and my family had ever tasted, so Dad and I were careful with each step.

First, we whisked together all the dry ingredients in one bowl. Then we mixed the wet ingredients using my stand mixer. We blended them all together, adding some hot water to the batter, and then dropped spoonfuls onto baking sheets. So far, so good.

"You know, I still remember the first dessert you baked all by yourself."

"Really?"

"Yeah. You were around six years old. You insisted upon doing everything yourself, even using the oven. We told you that we had to help you with that step, but you could do everything else."

"I sort of remember that . . ." I said. "What did I bake again?"

"Cookies. I can't remember the exact recipe, but it included sprinkles. The sprinkles got *everywhere*. But the cookies came out delicious. I know I took pictures. Let me see if I can find them." Dad grabbed his phone and opened his photo app.

While he looked, I slid the pan of cookies into the oven, put away the ingredients we no longer needed, and wiped off the counter so we'd have a clean space to make the filling.

"Ah, here they are." Dad showed me his phone.

There I was, a small Zoe standing in front of our oven, holding a plate of sprinkle-covered cookies. "I remember that apron." It'd had purple polka dots and I'd gotten it for Christmas. The next few photos were close-ups of the cookies, and then selfies with me and Dad, and Mom, Dad, and me together.

I really did have the best parents.

"It's amazing to see how you've developed as a baker," Dad said. "Anyway, what's next?"

"Let's make the filling," I said.

We creamed together butter and sugar and whipped it until it was fluffy. We added vanilla and folded in some marshmallow creme. Then we put it into the fridge to chill.

"How's your podcast going?" Dad asked while we cleaned up. "Your first episode was fantastic."

"Thanks." I grinned. "I read somewhere that for a brand-new podcast, twenty-six downloads for a first episode are pretty good. And I'm at fifty downloads already! Claire shared the episode with her coworkers, so that helped."

"I'm not surprised that you're already exceeding expectations."

"I hope it continues. Mom and I finished editing the next episode yesterday. We interviewed an exoneree. Just wait until you hear his story. And this is only the beginning. All of these stories need to be heard."

"They will," Dad said. "I can't wait to listen."

When the oven timer went off, we took the whoopie pies out and let them cool. That was another baking mistake—not letting your desserts cool enough before frosting them.

We scooped our fluffy filling into piping bags, and I carefully piped it onto half the cookies. Then Dad and I gently placed the other cookie half on top.

"They look really good!" I said. When I cut into one of them, I could see how moist the cookie was. I handed half to Dad and we both took bites.

"Wow," Dad said.

The whoopie pie melted in my mouth. The cookie was soft and decadent, and the filling was sweet and addictive. "We nailed it."

I took a picture of the whoopie pies with my phone and texted it to Trevor.

Less than five minutes later, there was a knock on our door. Trevor was on the other side when I opened it, and I led him to the kitchen.

"It smells amazing in here," Trevor said. "My mouth is already watering."

I handed him a small plate with his own whoopie pie on it. "Be honest," I said. "Rate it out of ten."

"Okay," Trevor said. He picked up the whoopie pie and inspected it from all angles. "Already, this looks a lot better than the other one. I give the presentation a . . . nine out of ten."

"Why not a ten?" I asked.

"It's a little lopsided."

I rolled my eyes at him. "Okay, but how does it taste?"

When Trevor took a bite, his eyes lit up. "This . . . is . . . *amazing.*"

"Better than the other one you had?"

"A million times better. One hundred out of ten."

I grinned. "Wow, thanks."

"You should serve these on the food truck," Trevor said. "They'd sell out in a second."

"You think so?"

"Yeah. Can I take a couple home with me?"

"Sure." We'd made over a dozen, so we'd still have plenty for Sunday dinner.

Trevor wrapped a couple of whoopie pies in a paper towel, and after he left, Dad and I finished cleaning up the rest of the kitchen.

"Thanks for asking me to bake with you," Dad said. "It's nice to spend this time together. I can't believe how fast you're growing up. It feels like you were just that little girl with the sprinkles cookies. And now you'll be in high school in one month."

"I'll still be home. It's not like I'm going off to college."

"I know. But you're becoming more and more independent. Look at you—you're starting a podcast and a food truck! It's remarkable. You're remarkable."

"Dad . . ." I said, feeling my cheeks get warm.

"It's true."

I paused cleaning, realizing I needed to get something off my chest. "I know I already apologized for inviting Marcus to J.P. Licks, but I wanted to also say that I'm sorry I've been spending more time with him, that it's taken away from our time together."

"Oh, Zoe. I don't want you to feel bad about that. Of course you should spend time with Marcus. He missed out on so much of your life, and you deserve to get to know your . . . father." He cleared his throat.

"You're my dad," I said. "Marcus is . . . Marcus. Big Tomato." I didn't know how else to explain it, but I knew in that moment that calling Marcus "Dad" just didn't feel right.

"I know that," Dad said. "I'll admit, I do miss our time together sometimes, but moments like these make up for it."

I gave Dad a big hug and felt a huge sense of relief.

Our chocolate whoopie pies were a hit at Sunday dinner. I was glad I made them, but they still didn't feel unique enough to be a signature dessert for our food truck. Maybe I could figure out a way to take them up a notch. Or I'd have to keep thinking of other ideas.

After dessert, I checked on our Kickstarter progress.

We were now at 23 percent of our goal, with three weeks to go. If we kept up this pace, it would be tight, but we could make it.

There was still hope.

Transcript Excerpt from
On Air with Zoe Washington **Episode 2**
Interview with Christopher Jackson, exoneree
Published on Monday, August 8

Zoe: I think a lot of people assume it's all sunshine and rainbows when an innocent person is finally freed from prison. That the hard part is over, so everything should get easier. But that's not true for a lot of exonerees. Has that been true for you?

Christopher: Listen, I wish it was all sunshine and rainbows. But it's been hard. At first it felt amazing to be out. I was finally free. I could finally do what I wanted, eat what I wanted, go where I wanted. But then I realized that things were not the same as before I was locked up. *I* wasn't the same.

Zoe: What about you wasn't the same?

Christopher: Prison messed me up. Being there, knowing I hadn't done anything wrong, gave me PTSD.

Zoe: Can you explain what PTSD is?

Christopher: It stands for post-traumatic stress disorder. A therapist diagnosed me with it sometime after I was released. I was on edge all the time. I couldn't sleep well or eat well or focus. I was terrified of getting locked up again for no reason. I had trouble trusting people, even family members.

Zoe: That sounds really hard.

Christopher: It is. One time I was out shopping with a friend to get some clothes. The person at the checkout forgot to take that device off a pair of shorts—you know, the white plastic thing that makes the alarm go off? Well, the alarm went off as we were leaving the store, and I immediately threw my hands up. I kept saying, "I didn't do it," over and over. I was completely freaked out.

Zoe: Wow. I'm so sorry.

Christopher: I'm getting help. But people need to understand that you don't only lose your freedom when you're wrongfully convicted. You lose a piece of yourself. The part that feels safe. It's like my body was finally free but my mind still wasn't.

And it's not that easy to get that part of yourself back.

Chapter Twenty-Eight

With everything going on—working at the bakery, recording my podcast interviews, and watching our Kickstarter donation page like a hawk—I felt busier than ever.

On Saturday, which was day fourteen of our Kickstarter, almost exactly halfway to our deadline, we were only at 40 percent of our goal: $12,000. I had been hoping to be at 50 percent or more by then. But there was still time. Maybe more people would donate closer to the deadline. Lots of people waited until the last minute to do things.

I had plans that day to hang out with Hannah. I was

excited to see her and do something fun for the afternoon. We'd texted and video chatted a bunch but hadn't seen each other in person since she came over to bake macarons, and that had been a few weeks ago. This time, we met up at a shopping center between our two houses that had a movie theater and some restaurants and shops.

We decided to see a movie first, so we went inside and got our tickets, a huge bucket of popcorn, and sodas.

"My mom wrote me back," Hannah said once we were settled into our seats. They were the comfy leather kind that reclined, so we both had our feet up. "The letter came yesterday."

"Oh, really?" I said. "Did you read it? What'd she say?"

"Not yet," Hannah said. "But I brought it with me. Will you watch me read it?"

"Right now?" I asked, looking around the theater. There actually weren't a lot of people in here, probably since we were at a matinee, and it was nice outside. The only other people in our row were across the room. It was quiet in here too, since the previews hadn't started yet, and the lights were still on.

"Is that okay?" Hannah asked. "I'm kind of nervous."

"Aww. Sure, of course."

Hannah took the letter out of her bag. Her hands shook a little as she smoothed the envelope out on her lap. I scooted closer to her so I could look at it. Hannah's mom's handwriting wasn't as neat as Marcus's, but otherwise the envelope looked really similar to the ones Marcus sent me. It even had the same American flag stamp.

It brought me right back to how I felt when I got Marcus's first letter. Like I couldn't wait to open it, but I also might throw up.

"You've got this," I told Hannah in a low voice. "No matter what she says, I'm proud of you for telling her how you feel."

Hannah flashed a small smile, and then took a deep breath. "Okay. I'm doing it." She turned the envelope over and opened it. She quickly removed the paper from inside and unfolded it. It was like she was doing it fast so she wouldn't lose her nerve.

After another deep breath, she started reading. I sat there quietly and watched her, but I didn't try to read it myself. The letter took up one side of a piece of loose-leaf paper, plus part of the second side.

Hannah was quiet as she read, and she bit her lower lip. When she was done, she put the letter down on her lap.

"Are you okay?" I asked.

Hannah stared straight ahead. "Yeah. It wasn't bad."

"It wasn't?"

"She said she cried after she got my letter," Hannah said, looking at me. "And, you know, my first thought when I read that was 'that's not fair.' She shouldn't get to cry after reading how *she* hurt *me*. But then I read more, and she explained that it was a good thing. Reading how I felt in my own words was like a punch in her gut. She said she needed to read it, and she was glad I sent it."

"Wow," I said.

"For real," Hannah said with a sigh.

"Did she say anything else?" I asked.

Hannah nodded. "She said she wants to change. She wants to do everything she can to get clean, and never do anything illegal again. She wants this to be her last time in prison, ever."

"Do you believe her?" I asked.

"I want to. I really do. I guess we'll see. But I'm glad I did this. I'm glad I wrote to her."

"Are you going to write her back?"

"I think so." Hannah stared at the letter again. "I like talking to her this way. It gives me time to think about what I want to say. She can't interrupt me or talk over me, like she used to do. And it seems like she's listening." She shrugged. "We'll see how this goes."

I hoped that Hannah exchanging letters would bring her and her mom together, like it did for me and Marcus.

"So . . . you're okay?" I asked.

Hannah nodded tentatively. "I think so." She took a huge sip of her soda. "But I think I'm going to need some candy to go with this popcorn. Something chocolatey."

"I don't know what we were thinking, not buying some in the first place," I said.

"We made a huge mistake." Hannah tried to keep her serious face but cracked a little.

I stood up. "I'll go get some. My treat."

The previews had started by the time I got back to my seat with two bags of chocolate candy.

"Thanks," Hannah whispered when I passed her one of the bags. I knew she wasn't just talking about the chocolate.

"Anytime."

Later that weekend, I was looking at the notebook that I was using to jot down notes for my podcast. On one page was my list of people to interview. So far, everyone I'd interviewed was someone Marcus's lawyers had connected me to, or someone Marcus had met since getting out of prison himself.

Maybe I could interview Hannah's mom when she got out of prison. If she was telling Hannah the truth, she did want to change and do better. And it seemed like it might be challenging for her once she got out of prison. If it was hard for people who were actually innocent to get support and resources, I guessed that it'd be even harder for those who'd been guilty.

I had a feeling if I told Marcus about Hannah's mom, he'd say she was the kind of person he'd want to help, if she really did want a better life for herself. Then I wondered—if Marcus and I were able to open our food truck, would I be okay with us hiring Hannah's mom? Giving her a chance—like Ariana gave Marcus a chance—could make a big difference in Hannah getting her mom back. I wanted that for Hannah. If her mom proved that she wanted that too, then why shouldn't she get the help she needed?

I wasn't sure. I didn't even know Hannah's mom, if she'd really want to change her life for the better.

At the bottom of my list of people to interview, I added a note to look into interviewing previously incarcerated people who weren't exonerees. At the very least, it could be interesting to hear their perspective.

Maybe Marcus was on to something. Maybe I needed to be more open-minded.

Transcript Excerpt from
On Air with Zoe Washington Episode 3
Interview with Robert Wilson, exoneree
Published on Monday, August 15

Rob: Sometimes I feel like the unluckiest and luckiest man—at the same time. First I went to prison for thirty-one years for a crime I didn't commit. But then, when my conviction was overturned, I became a millionaire.

Zoe: How did you end up a millionaire?

Rob: The state of North Carolina awarded me $31 million in compensation for being wrongfully convicted. That's $1 million for each year that I was behind bars. But let me tell you, it wasn't an easy road to get here. My lawyer and I filed a federal civil rights lawsuit. I had to fight for years for this compensation. And in the process, it was like I had to defend my innocence all over again.

Zoe: Do you feel like it makes up for all those years you were behind bars?

Rob: Not at all. Money isn't everything.

Zoe: What do you mean by that?

Rob: I'd give all this money back to have a better relationship with my family. When I first got out, even though they knew I was exonerated, that I was innocent, they still looked at me different because I'd spent so many years behind bars. Things still aren't the same between us.

Zoe: I'm sorry to hear that.

Rob: I'm still grateful for the money, though. It doesn't fix everything, but it's allowed me to get back on my feet. And it means a lot to know that the state acknowledged they did something wrong by convicting me.

I hope more states will make it easier to get this compensation. Because getting our freedom back is not enough.

Chapter Twenty-Nine

A few days later, when I checked our Kickstarter page again, I started to feel anxious. We were now over halfway to our deadline, but at only 42 percent of our goal. The total raised was $12,600. Barely anyone had contributed during the last few days.

"I'm freaking out," I told my parents during dinner. The huge pit in my stomach made it hard to eat the spaghetti and garlic bread, even though it all smelled amazing.

"Is there anyone you haven't shared the link with yet?" I asked. "Are you sure you posted about it everywhere, and messaged it to everyone you know? Even at work?"

Mom and Dad both nodded.

"I sent it to everyone I could think of," Mom said. "And a lot of them have donated already."

"I'll share it with my coworkers again tomorrow," Dad said. "I can bring it up during our team meeting. But there's still time left, kiddo. You don't need to worry."

"I can't help it," I said. "I don't know if we're going to make our goal if only people we know are donating. We need people we don't know to donate, too." But how would I get strangers' attention? I needed the Kickstarter to go viral somehow.

"Zoe, honey," Mom said. "Take a breath."

She breathed in and out and I followed along. But I could only manage to take a shallow breath.

Then Mom said, "If for some reason the Kickstarter doesn't get funded, I hope you still feel proud of all of the work you've done."

My breath got caught in my throat again. "Don't even say that!" I said. "You don't think we're going to make our goal?"

"That's not what I'm saying," Mom said. "You can absolutely still make your goal. Just, no matter what happens, we're proud of you."

"I know," I said. "But this isn't making me feel better." I pushed my plate away. "I'm not hungry. Can I eat later?

I'm going to go to my room."

"I'll save your plate for you," Mom said.

I got up and started walking out of the kitchen to head upstairs.

"Zoe?" Mom asked.

I looked back at her.

"It's going to be okay. Whatever happens. I promise you that."

I nodded but wasn't sure I believed her.

Back in my room, I paced around and tried to calm down. But all I could think about was the Kickstarter failing and Marcus's and my dream not coming true. Not now, maybe not ever.

Maybe my parents had been right about lowering my expectations, back when I had first brought up the restaurant idea. Maybe this Kickstarter had always been a lost cause.

Maybe instead of forcing myself to remain hopeful, I needed to face reality.

Big and Little BBQ Truck was nothing but a pipe dream.

I slogged through the first few hours of work at Ari's Cakes the next day. We didn't have many customers, so I spent a lot of time refilling napkin dispensers, restocking our folded boxes, and feeling like I was a lopsided three-tiered cake about to topple over and splatter everywhere. I avoided the kitchen, which only reminded me that I wouldn't be baking in my own professional kitchen any-time soon. I also kept my phone buried in my bag so I wouldn't be tempted to check our Kickstarter again. There was no point.

I knew our Kickstarter wasn't technically over, but it felt over to me.

During our lunch break, Marcus suggested we check out more of the Black Heritage Trail landmarks. Three of them were on Pinckney Street, so we walked down it. It was super quaint, like out of a movie. It could only fit one lane of cars, and had brick sidewalks, townhomes on each side with flowers in window boxes, and lanterns instead of streetlamps. One of the trail landmarks was the Phillips School, one of Boston's first schools to integrate its student body after segregation was abolished in Massachusetts in 1855.

Each of the stops we visited were interesting, but I could barely focus on learning about them. Marcus must've been able to tell, because when we got to the end of the block, he suggested we find a place to sit and talk for a few minutes before heading back to Ari's Cakes.

"What's on your mind?" he asked once we found an empty bench.

There was no point in trying to hide my feelings from him. "Our Kickstarter isn't going well anymore," I said. "I feel like a failure."

I pulled up the Kickstarter page on my phone so he could see. We were still only at $12,600. My heart sank. I'd hoped while I was at work, a couple more donations would've come in. Maybe someone from Dad's job. But there was nothing new.

I sighed. "I'm the one who convinced you to start it in the first place, and nothing is working out. We don't even get to keep any of the donations that came in if the whole thing doesn't get funded. So we'll be back at square one."

"Listen. My Little Tomato." Marcus grabbed my hands in his. "No matter what happens, you are not a failure. You hear me?"

"You have to say that because I'm your daughter."

"I'm saying that because you're spectacular." Marcus gently lifted my chin to make me look at him. He was both serious and sincere when he said, "You're the epitome of Black Girl Magic."

I looked away and shook my head. I didn't feel like that at all.

"Think of everything you've accomplished so far. You're a talented baker at such a young age. Ariana still has your cupcake recipe for sale. How many other fourteen-year-olds can say that?

"But even more incredible," Marcus continued, "is that you are the reason I'm out of prison."

I gave Marcus a doubtful glare.

"I'm serious," he said. "You are the one who found Susan Thomas and pushed me to reach out to the Innocence Project. Before that, I'd given up. I had lost faith in the system and was waiting for parole, when maybe I could finally get out. But then you responded to my letter. And you gave me two of the biggest gifts of my life. Your words—in all the letters you wrote back to me. And hope.

"You got me exonerated, Zoe. You did that. I'd still be in prison right now if it wasn't for you."

"You're going to make me cry," I said in a quiet voice.

Marcus put his arm around my shoulder. "You can do literally anything you put your mind to. You have the power to make change. You've done it for me already! And you know, me getting out of prison was just the beginning. Now I have my whole life ahead of me. And you have even more life ahead of you.

"I know, even if this Kickstarter doesn't work out, that

we will open a restaurant one day. Even if it takes more time, it will happen. And it's okay if it takes some time. Because we will be on this journey together. You're not alone in this."

I leaned my head on Marcus's shoulder and wiped my watery eyes.

"Okay," I finally said.

Marcus got up and I did the same.

"Before we go, I want to hear you say it. 'I am spectacular.' Say it."

"Marcus . . ." I said. "Let's just head back."

"Not until you say it."

"Fine . . ." I mumbled, "I'm spectacular."

Marcus put his hand behind his ear. "What's that? I couldn't hear you."

"I'm spectacular," I said a little louder.

"One more time, with feeling," Marcus said, raising his voice.

"I'm spectacular!" I half shouted. A couple of people walking by paused to look at me, but I ignored them and smiled.

"Don't you forget it."

Chapter Thirty

My conversation with Marcus made me feel a lot better. He was right—we were in this together, and the Kickstarter wasn't the only way to make our dream come true.

I still really wanted it to be funded. But I couldn't sit around and wait for more funders to appear. I had to find them somehow.

When I got home from work, I thought of an idea. On my laptop, I dug through old emails until I found the response from Boston Public Radio last month, when they said they couldn't do the exoneree interview series. I clicked Reply and started to type.

Dear Tyler,

Thanks for responding to my email. I ended up starting my own podcast, called *On Air with Zoe Washington*, so I could interview exonerees myself. It's going well. But that's not why I'm writing.

Marcus and I started a Kickstarter to raise funds to open our own food truck. It's a big dream of ours to do this together. I was wondering if you could add the link to the page on your website where listeners can find our interview. Maybe you can re-share our interview and this link on social media?

Thanks for considering!

Sincerely,

Zoe Washington

I pasted in the link to our Kickstarter page and hit Send. I wasn't sure that the radio station would agree to help, but it was worth a try.

In the meantime, I had to come up with some other ideas to get the word out about our Kickstarter. Maybe I could dedicate an entire episode of my podcast to it. But my audience wasn't that big yet. It was mostly people I knew, who'd already donated.

And then I remembered something that I'd heard recently.

On my laptop, I looked up the website for my favorite baking podcast, *The Sweetest Podcast*. They'd announced something in their last episode. There it was, right on top of the website: information about their first live podcast event happening next month. It was going to take place in New York City, so I wouldn't get to go, but I read the details. It was going to include interviews with two well-known pastry chefs live onstage, as well as baking demos. The interview part of the event would be recorded and air on the podcast later, but people could buy tickets to watch it live, and ask the chefs questions. It sounded *really* cool, and I wished I could go.

But more importantly, it gave me an idea. What if I made my podcast into a live event? Instead of interviewing another exoneree on a video call like I'd been doing so far, I could see if someone would be willing to be interviewed live, in front of an audience. Even better, I could interview more than one person, like as a panel. I didn't have the technology to record a live event to post on my podcast, but that was okay. It could just be available live.

Instead of selling tickets, we could take donations that could go toward our Kickstarter. Maybe Marcus could even cook some of the barbecue that'll be available on our truck and give out samples. I could also give out dessert samples.

Not only could this event raise money for our Kickstarter, but it could also raise more awareness around the injustices that exonerees experience. That awareness could lead to change. And then it could help not only Marcus and me, but so many other people.

The more I thought about it, the more I wanted to do it. But already, I could think of four challenges:

1. Where would we hold an event like this? If we were able to get a lot of people to come, we'd need a big enough space.

2. How would we get people to come? Especially people in the community who we didn't know?

3. The Kickstarter deadline was in less than two weeks. Could we really plan and publicize an event in time?

4. Could we do this without spending a lot of money—which we didn't have?

This sounded impossible. I bet *The Sweetest Podcast* team had planned their live event for months—and had a big budget. There were probably other challenges I hadn't even thought of yet.

But I still really, really wanted to try.

First, I had to get Marcus and my parents on board. If they didn't agree to help me, there was no way I could pull it off on my own.

I couldn't wait until Sunday dinner to get everyone together, so I messaged Marcus and then told my parents that we needed to have a family meeting that night.

"Hey, Little T. What's going on?" Marcus asked once I got him on video chat. I could tell that he was sitting at the table in Grandma's kitchen.

"Hi, Zoe," Grandma said from off camera. She must've also been in the kitchen, but I couldn't see her on Marcus's phone screen.

"Hey, Marcus. Hi, Grandma," I said. "One second, just waiting for Mom and Dad."

I called out to them and let them know I was ready.

They joined me in the living room and sat next to me on the couch.

"I came up with an idea to fund the rest of the Kickstarter," I said. "Since we're getting so close to the deadline, and still need a lot of donations." I paused before saying, "I want to put together a live podcast event."

"A what?" Marcus said from the other end of the video call.

"What does that mean, exactly?" Mom asked.

I told them about *The Sweetest Podcast*'s event coming up, and all my ideas for a live *On Air with Zoe Washington* fundraiser event.

"Here's the thing," I added. "It'd need to be a week from this Saturday or Sunday. Because the Kickstarter deadline is the following Monday."

"You want to plan a live event in a week?" Dad asked.

"A week plus a couple of days," I said, but Dad's doubtful expression didn't change. "I know it sounds impossible. Maybe we can't pull it off. But I feel like I must try. I can't let our Kickstarter fail. Not without a fight."

"That's my girl," Grandma said from somewhere in the background of Marcus's video. It made me chuckle since I still couldn't see her.

Mom shook her head. "I don't know, Zoe. I have no idea how we'd organize an event like this in such a short time."

"I made a list of things to do to start," I said. "First, we'd need to find a venue. Maybe we can see if the library will let us rent their event room?"

"We can ask," Mom said. "But it's last minute, so it may already be booked. And it usually costs money to rent space."

"Plus, the library probably wouldn't let you serve food," Dad added. "So you wouldn't be able to give out samples."

I hadn't thought of that. "Okay, so we'll find another space. There's got to be a place we can use for free, or really cheap."

I realized Marcus hadn't said anything yet. "What do you think, Big T? Is this idea too bananas?"

He let out a breath. "I honestly don't know, Little T. But listen, if you want to try, I'm in."

I grinned.

"Like I said to you before," Marcus continued, "you can do anything you put your mind to. Let's do it. Let's plan an event."

I looked at Mom and Dad. "Do I have your permission? And can you help? Please?"

They looked at each other and had a silent conversation with their eyes.

"I mean," Mom said to me, "if you and Marcus really want to do this, we'll help however we can. But this is not going to be easy, Zoe. It may not work out."

"I know that," I said. "No matter what happens, at least I'll know I tried."

"Just let me know where and when to show up, baby," Grandma's voice said. At least she was optimistic.

Marcus and I stayed on the phone for the next hour . making a list of action steps. We decided to have the event on the Saturday before the Kickstarter deadline, instead of that Sunday, so hopefully more people would be available. That gave us nine days to make it happen.

Nine days and a lot of work to do.

The countdown was on.

Chapter Thirty-One

The first thing we had to do was nail down a venue. If we couldn't find a place for people to gather, then we couldn't have a live event.

During my lunch break on Thursday, I looked up how to rent event space at our local library, in case they did have a room available. I figured if we had it there, the library might be able to help us advertise to the community. But on their website, I saw that it cost $500 to rent one of their large event rooms for a few hours. Our whole reason for doing this was to *raise* money, not to spend lots of it. Anyway, when I looked at the library calendar, I saw something was already scheduled for the following Saturday.

As soon as my workday was over, I grabbed my backpack and got right back on my phone. I started looking up other event spaces in the area. I was still staring at different websites while Grandma drove me home. Banquet halls were too expensive and restaurant party rooms wouldn't fit enough people. Maybe we could use the auditorium or gym at one of the schools in town. I went to the Medford Public Schools website to start looking for information.

"How are you feeling, Zoe?" Grandma asked. "You seem stressed."

I answered without looking up from my phone screen. "I am stressed. I really want this event to work out."

"Well, you can't spend the next week worrying yourself sick over this. It's not healthy. Just take it one step at a time."

"I'll try." I needed a break, so I put my phone away and stared out the window instead. I leaned against it, feeling like I could easily fall asleep. I hadn't slept well the night before since I was too jittery thinking about everything Marcus and I had to do.

When we were back in Medford, not far from home, I saw something out of Grandma's car window that made me sit up straight. "Wait! Grandma, can you pull over?"

* * *

I'd spotted the bandshell. In the same park where the farmers market took place each week, there was an outdoor bandshell with a stage. Sometimes bands played live music there, and the city also hosted summer movie nights there. Across from the stage was a big grassy area where people could bring their own blankets and seats. I'd completely forgotten about it until I saw it from out of Grandma's window.

She parked the car in the lot, and we walked over to the stage to get a closer look. It'd been cloudy and lightly raining all day, so nobody was around, except for a couple of people walking their dogs.

"What if we did it here?" I asked Grandma.

"It's a nice space," she said. "Has a stage already and everything."

"Wait here," I said, and walked around the side of the bandshell so I could get onto the stage. "There's plenty of space up here," I yelled down to Grandma. "But we might need microphones or something . . ."

I looked out at all the grass in front of the stage. A hundred or more people could fit here. If everyone brought their own seats or blankets, we wouldn't have to pay for chairs.

I went back down to where Grandma was standing.

"The only thing to think about is weather," she said.

"If it rained, people sitting in the grassy area wouldn't be covered."

"True." I pulled out my phone and opened the weather app. As of today, it said the following Saturday would be partly cloudy and eighty degrees. If the forecast stayed that way, it'd be perfect. I snapped a couple of pictures of the stage and areas around it to send to Marcus, and then Grandma and I walked back to her car.

At home, I found the website with information on how to use the bandshell for an event. Anyone was allowed to use it as long as they applied for a permit with the Medford parks and recreation department. There was an application right on the website, and an email address where it could be sent. The permit cost wasn't on the website, so we'd have to ask about that. I hoped it was cheaper than the other event spaces I'd found online. The good news was I didn't see anything listed for that Saturday evening on the park events calendar, so it looked like the bandshell was available. But the site listed one other requirement to rent the space: all the events had to be free to the public.

Our event was technically going to be free, and we wanted as much of the public to come as possible. We were just hoping to be able to collect Kickstarter donations. I wondered if doing that would go against the rules.

I explained all of this to Marcus over the phone. He said he'd call the parks and recreation department the next day during his lunch break at the legal nonprofit and ask all our questions. I crossed my fingers that they would allow us to take donations during our event, because this space was perfect, and it already felt like we were running out of time.

Chapter Thirty-Two

On Friday during lunch, I kept my phone near me in case Marcus called from his other job. I felt so antsy that I ended up taking a walk around Beacon Hill to get my nervous energy out.

Finally, ten minutes before my break was over, my phone vibrated, and Marcus's face appeared on the screen.

"Hey!" I said once I picked up. "Did you talk to them? What did they say?"

"I just got off the phone with someone at the parks and rec department," Marcus said. "She confirmed that the bandshell is free that night. We could start the event at four p.m."

My whole body exhaled. "Great! What else did she say?"

"I explained what our event was about, and how we wanted to take donations for our Kickstarter."

Marcus paused for a second and I said, "And?"

He laughed. "I'm getting to it, Little T. They said the only rule was we couldn't charge for the event. People have to be able to show up and watch our panel without paying for anything."

"Oh," I said, thinking that this was the end of it.

"That's not all," Marcus said. "She said if we want to talk about the Kickstarter and let people know they can donate, as long as it's optional, it's fine."

"Okay!" I said. "We can work with that. I was thinking, maybe we could print out flyers about the Kickstarter and hand them out at the event. We could print QR codes on them so people can easily get to the Kickstarter website from their phones."

"I have no idea what a QR code is, but sure," Marcus said. "Sounds good."

"I'll show it to you later." Then I thought of something. "Wait, how much is the permit?"

"It's only fifty dollars to apply for the permit. The lady on the phone says if we get it in today, they can process it on Monday, so we'll be all set."

I couldn't believe this was working out so well!

"There's one thing they said we can't do," Marcus added.

Maybe I had spoken too soon. "What?" I asked.

"We can't serve our samples. Since we don't have a permit for our food truck yet, and we're not an official restaurant business, we're not allowed to serve our food."

"That stinks." I'd been looking forward to sharing dessert samples, even if I still hadn't figured out my signature dessert.

"But they said if we wanted to bring in any other food vendor, that was fine—they just need to have a permit." He paused. "I was thinking, maybe we can ask Ariana to donate some of her cupcakes to the cause, and we can give those out."

"That's a good idea! She has those mini cupcakes, which would be perfect."

"Right," Marcus said. "I'll fill out this permit application now and send it over."

"Does this mean we officially have a venue?" I said, barely able to contain my excitement.

"This means we officially have a venue."

"Yes!" I did a happy dance right in the middle of the

sidewalk. "I'll ask Ariana about donating cupcakes when I get back inside. And then we have to . . . you know . . . plan everything else!"

Now we *had* to book our panelists. Otherwise, I'd be standing on that bandshell stage in front of an audience all by myself. The thought made me want to break out into hives. I was already nervous about doing this event since I'd never done anything like this before. But at least I wouldn't have to be onstage alone.

I'd been thinking a lot about who to invite. It'd be good to have not only people who'd been wrongfully imprisoned, but also a lawyer or someone else who works to support them. That way we could get multiple perspectives on the issue. Marcus agreed to ask around, since he was in touch with other exonerees.

Before I went back to work, I quickly sent an email to Claire, the Innocence Project lawyer who I'd already interviewed on my podcast. I asked if she or anyone else at the Innocence Project could join the panel. I explained that we didn't have much time to plan, and could she get back to me on Monday?

I also emailed Christopher Jackson and Robert Wilson, my other two podcast guests, to see if they could recommend anyone else.

On Saturday, Marcus called to say he had good news. "I have someone who agreed to be a panelist at our event. And where she works has a big network, so she could help spread the word."

"What! That's amazing!" I said. "Who is it?"

"Her name is Christina Stone. She works for an organization called Fresh Start, and they provide re-entry services. They help former offenders get the support they need after incarceration, like housing, jobs, and education. When I told her about our event, she was very enthusiastic and eager to help."

"That's great," I said. "But wait, former offenders? Does that mean they were guilty of their crimes?"

"Yes," Marcus said. "That's how I first met her. I've been talking to her about how I'd love to meet some of the people she works with and see about hiring a couple of them for our truck."

A pit grew in my stomach. "But my podcast has been about interviewing exonerees. Not people who actually committed crimes."

"I know, but since this is a panel, I thought she could bring a different perspective. She has a lot of insight to share about what it's like for people after prison."

"I don't know . . ."

"Little T." The way he said my nickname, and the way

237

he paused right after, it was like he had something on his mind and was figuring out how to say it. "You know that not all people who've committed crimes are bad people, right?"

"Yeah," I said. "I mean, I guess." I remembered back when I still thought Marcus might be guilty of his crime, and how I tried to figure out how he could seem so kind but have done something so terrible. But in the end, he *was* innocent.

"Well, I'll tell you—they aren't," Marcus said. "There are so many reasons why people commit crimes, and it's not always because they're bad. I already told you about my friend Shawn. There are so many other people like him out there."

I sighed. "I know. I don't know why it still makes me nervous to think of you hiring someone like that to work on our truck. I know it means a lot to you, but I'm still not sure."

"I know exactly why you feel that way, and it's because society makes you think, 'once a convict, always a convict.' There's a big misconception that people cannot change. And a huge stigma about being in prison. Even I'm dealing with that stigma, and I didn't even deserve to be in there.

"But people *can* change, Zoe. I've seen it with my own

eyes—men who I got to know in prison who did terrible things, but you wouldn't even know it based on how they talked and behaved when I met them, years after the fact. They'd done the hard work of going through personal growth and change. And they deserve support when they get out, too."

I thought of Hannah's mom. Didn't she deserve support so she could be a good mom again?

"Listen," Marcus said. "I won't force you to add Christina to the panel. But I think if she's there, you'll get a lot out of what she has to say. Your whole audience will. Why don't you think about it, and we can let her know one way or the other on Monday? You can do your own research too. I'll send you her information."

I agreed to think about it. But part of me hoped we'd find other panelists so I wouldn't actually have to.

Chapter Thirty-Three

Marcus and I decided to cancel our next Sunday dinner so instead of cooking all day, we could finish preparing for our event. It was a good thing too, because on Sunday morning, I woke up with an amazing idea. Since our town's farmers market took place in the same park as the bandshell, we could hand out flyers to spread the word about the event to people who live in the area.

The only problem was that the market started at ten a.m., and by the time I woke up with this idea, it was after nine a.m. The market ended at one.

We also didn't have any flyers ready to hand out. Could I quickly put something together?

It was worth a try. I jumped out of bed and moved over to my desk, where I got to work designing a flyer. But as soon as I opened a blank document on my laptop, I realized that I only knew the place and time of our event, but not exactly who would be there. Besides me. And Marcus.

I wouldn't let that stop me. I added my podcast logo to the top of the page, and then below it, wrote "On Air with Zoe Washington . . . LIVE!" Already it looked pretty cool. I still couldn't believe I'd started my own podcast.

Below that I wrote:

Come to this FREE event and learn
about life AFTER incarceration!

Join host Zoe Washington and a panel of guests for an
informative and important panel discussion all about
how and why people who've been wrongfully imprisoned
struggle once they're finally free, and how you can help.

Saturday, August 27, at 4 p.m. at the Medford bandshell
Bring your own blanket or chair. All are welcome!

All the information was there, but it still needed something to draw people in. Then I remembered that Ariana had agreed to donate mini cupcakes and lemonade. In even bigger letters at the bottom, I wrote:

***FREE cupcakes and lemonade from
Boston's own Ari's Cakes for all attendees!***

Next to that, I pasted in the Ari's Cakes logo.

I wondered if I should mention the Kickstarter on the flyer or wait until the actual event. The fundraiser was the reason why we were doing this, but donating was supposed to be optional for us to use the bandshell. I decided it wouldn't hurt to add the QR code in the corner of the flyer. If anyone got curious and opened it, they could see what our Kickstarter was all about and decide whether they wanted to contribute. Maybe some people would donate before next weekend! A quick Google search showed me how to turn our Kickstarter link into a QR code image, which I pasted into the corner of the page.

Once that was done, I printed off one copy. Looking it over, I decided it wasn't bad for a last-minute design.

I brought it to the kitchen to show my parents. Mom was sitting down in her bathrobe, drinking coffee, and Dad was at the stove cooking scrambled eggs and bacon.

"Morning, kiddo," Dad said. "Breakfast is almost ready."

Eating was the last thing on my mind. I put the flyer on the table in front of Mom. "Can we make a bunch of copies of this and hand them out at the farmers market?" I glanced at the clock on the microwave. The market began in a few minutes. "Like, now? I can pay for the copies."

"This looks nice," Mom said about the flyer. "We can go hand them out after we eat breakfast."

"Do we have to eat first? Can't we go now?"

"No. Your dad is in the middle of cooking. And do you want me to be hangry?" Mom asked.

I glanced at the pans of food on the stove, and then back at Mom. I'd seen her when she was hangry before and it was not fun. "Okay, fine."

While Dad finished up breakfast, I went next door to ask Trevor if he was free to come with us and help hand out the flyers. He agreed, and we also messaged Maya on our group text. She agreed too. This would be my first time seeing her and Trevor together since our bowling night. For the first time since I'd found out they liked each other, I wasn't worried about being a third wheel. I knew we were all still friends and was glad they were both willing to help.

By the time my parents and I finished eating breakfast and got dressed, Maya had come over.

"Thanks for coming!" I gave her a hug.

"Anything for my bestie," Maya said, which made my heart squeeze.

Mom, Dad, Trevor, Maya, and I all piled into the car.

First, we went to a nearby printing place and printed off a couple hundred copies. It was worth the extra money to print the flyers in color. They actually looked pretty professional!

When we arrived at the farmers market, it was 11:17 a.m. There were plenty of people out shopping, maybe more than if we'd come right when the market opened.

"Let's split up to hand them out," I said.

We agreed to meet by the bandshell once all our flyers were gone.

I started walking toward the corner of the market, where there were vegetable stands. "Free event, next weekend," I said as I passed out my first flyer. "Right at the bandshell. There will be free cupcakes, too!"

I did this repeatedly for the next hour.

Not everyone wanted to take a flyer, but most of them did. A few people seemed like they might be interested, from the look on their face when they read the piece of paper. But as I walked to the bandshell once all my flyers were gone, I noticed a few in a garbage can, or left behind on park benches.

Mom and Trevor were already at the bandshell.

"How'd it go?" I asked them.

"Fine," Mom said. "I had a nice conversation with someone who said she'd come."

"That's great!" I said.

Dad and Maya joined us a couple minutes later.

"Do you think this made a difference?" I asked as we all walked back to the car.

"I'm sure it did," Dad said.

I hoped that enough people kept the flyer or saved the information and wanted to come and learn.

Not only because I wanted people to help our Kickstarter. But because this *was* an important conversation, and it was about time our community had it, together.

Chapter Thirty-Four

Back home, I started to wish we hadn't canceled Sunday dinner. I'd gotten used to the routine of baking a new dessert every Sunday. Now it felt strange not to.

If I wasn't going to bake, I could at least brainstorm more ideas for my signature dessert. I liked the whoopie pies I'd baked, and they seemed like the perfect food truck dessert since they were handheld and portable. We could sell either one regular-sized whoopie pie, or maybe three mini whoopie pies.

Maybe we could roll out different flavors depending on the season. In the fall, we could have a pumpkin flavor. For winter, we could do chocolate peppermint or gingerbread. In the spring, we could make a lavender vanilla flavor, and lemon for summer, maybe with blueberry or raspberry added.

I still wanted to come up with a signature flavor that we could sell year-round, and that people could associate with our truck. But what?

I thought about all the desserts I'd made that summer—chocolate and cherry brownies, key lime pie, pineapple upside-down cake, strawberry shortcake, macarons, and beignets. Clearly, I liked baking with fruit. But which dessert was my favorite?

I closed my eyes and thought about the best bite I'd had in the last couple of months. The dessert I'd want to eat again, right that second if I could.

What came to my mind surprised me.

The best bite I'd tasted that summer wasn't something that I'd baked myself. It was actually the red velvet cake ice cream from J.P. Licks. It was so delicious; I'd eat an entire pint right now if I could.

I didn't want my signature dessert to be ice cream, but it was the perfect inspiration. A picture materialized in my mind, like on *Kids Bake Challenge!* when they showed a professional sketch of a dessert on the screen while the contestant described what they were planning to make.

I texted Maya and Trevor in our group chat.

ME: Would you eat a red velvet whoopie pie filled with
    cream cheese frosting and crushed up toasted
    pecans?

Right away, three dots appeared next to Trevor's name.

TREVOR: Absolutely I'll be right over
ME: Wait I haven't made them yet!
TREVOR: Stop playing with my emotions
MAYA: 🍪
MAYA: That sounds yummy

If it hadn't been Sunday night, I would have asked my
parents to take me to the grocery store right then.

ME: Baking them tomorrow. They might be my new
    signature dessert. Want to come over after dinner
    to try them?
TREVOR: Duh
MAYA: Yup! Can't wait
MAYA: How'd you come up with that?

I explained how Dad had introduced me to the red
velvet cake ice cream flavor. That was another reason

why I was excited about this idea. It was a way to make Dad a tiny part of this food truck. A way to show him that even though I was opening this truck with Marcus, he was still important to me.

The ice cream at J.P. Licks didn't have any pecans—just the red velvet cake pieces, vanilla ice cream, and swirls of cream cheese frosting. But when I'd made the regular chocolate whoopie pies, the one thing I felt it was missing was something with texture. Something crunchy.

I'd learned from watching hours and hours of baking shows that adding some crunch to soft desserts makes them that much tastier. The pecans would add texture and flavor.

Maybe this recipe wouldn't be as unique or surprising as my Froot Loop cupcakes, but it felt right. I hoped they tasted right too.

It was hard to concentrate the next day at Ari's Cakes. I kept thinking about the red velvet whoopie pies I was going to bake after work. When I wasn't thinking about that, I was stressing over the fact that we were five days from our live podcast event and still didn't have any panelists lined up.

As soon as my lunch break started, I went to my phone

to see if anyone had responded to my emails. When I saw an email from Claire, I immediately opened it. But my excitement fizzled out when I read that she wasn't going to be available. She said she'd ask around to see if anyone else in her office could participate.

Ugh. What if nobody else was free? Marcus hadn't had any luck finding anyone within his exoneree community to join the event. There was one person who'd agreed to be interviewed for a future episode of my podcast but didn't feel comfortable appearing live onstage.

I ate my lunch, and then since there was time left, I went on a walk to get my anxious energy out. As soon as I got outside, I took out my phone and called Hannah.

"Hey!" Hannah said when she picked up. "Aren't you at work?"

"It's my lunch break. I've been feeling stressed all morning, so I'm taking a walk. Then I called you because it turns out I can walk and stress at the same time."

"Sorry. Is it about the event on Saturday? I can come, by the way. My dad said he'll take me."

"Awesome!" I said. "I hope it won't be only me on the stage."

"Did the other people drop out or something?"

"There aren't any other people, not yet. I've been

telling everyone we're having a panel, but we don't have any panelists lined up yet. Except for Marcus. One person I wanted just emailed me to say she's not available."

"Oh no. Does that mean you have to cancel the event?"

"I hope not," I said. "Worst-case scenario, Marcus knows one person who could do it."

"That's great!"

"I guess. It's just not the kind of panelist I was hoping for."

"What do you mean?" Hannah asked.

I explained who Christina was, and how her job didn't exactly fit the theme for this event—life after incarceration for *exonerees*.

"I get that," Hannah said. "But she still knows about the struggles people experience after prison, right? So, she'd still be able to spread awareness."

"That's true."

"I wonder what she'd say," Hannah admitted. "Maybe she could help my mom when she gets out."

"She probably could." Now that Hannah brought up her mom, I was kind of curious too.

"I don't think I told you this," I said, "but Marcus wants to hire a previous offender to work on our food truck. Like someone who committed a crime, served their time, and is out now and wants to start fresh."

"That's cool," Hannah said.

"You think so?"

"Yeah. I mean, I hope that's what my mom will want to do. And I hope she can find a place to work that'll support her."

I wanted that for Hannah and her mom, too.

"Do you think it matters what kind of crime someone committed?" I asked. "Like, if someone committed a violent crime and wanted a second chance after they got out of prison, do they deserve that?"

"Hmm." There was a long pause before Hannah spoke again. "Honestly, I don't know. I guess it depends on the person and the crime. But I want to believe that people can change. Because if people can't, then that means my mom can't change. And I desperately want her to."

"That makes sense. Did you reply to her last letter?"

"Yup. And I told her about you, too."

"Really?"

"Yeah. I wrote about your relationship with Marcus, and said you inspired me to write letters to her."

"Aww, that's so nice." I checked the time on my phone screen. "I have to head back inside, but thanks for talking to me."

"Of course."

"You inspire me too, you know," I added. "I'm so glad you found me at the bakery."

We said goodbye and I walked back into Ari's Cakes feeling a little better.

Chapter Thirty-Five

I'd made red velvet cake plenty of times before and knew that even though it had a chocolatey flavor, it wasn't the same as chocolate cake. Besides the unsweetened cocoa powder and other typical cake ingredients, it also had buttermilk and vinegar. They were what made red velvet cakes taste slightly tangy. And, of course, you had to add food coloring to give it the perfect red color.

Whoopie pie and cake recipes weren't the same, but they were similar enough. So, when I got home from work, I used what I knew about red velvet cake to modify the chocolate whoopie pie recipe that I'd made with Dad.

I mixed up the batter, adding buttermilk and vinegar.

Then I dropped spoonfuls onto a baking sheet and slid it into the oven. While they baked, I made the cream cheese frosting, tasting it and adjusting the ingredients to make sure the flavor and texture were just right.

When the whoopie pies were done, I took them out of the oven to cool. Then I got started on the last component: the toasted pecans. I dropped some pecans onto a different baking sheet, lined with parchment paper, and let them bake in the oven for eight minutes. Once they were done and cooled off, I chopped them up using my food processor. From the smell alone, I could tell that toasting the pecans made them much more flavorful.

Finally, it was time to assemble the sandwiches. Between two whoopie pie pieces, I piped cream cheese frosting and added a layer of toasted pecans. Once the pies were all assembled, I put them on a platter and sprinkled some confectioners' sugar on top, to make them look more festive.

They looked great, and only took about an hour to make. I didn't think it'd be too hard to make larger batches for our food truck, especially if I used Ariana's kitchen.

But how did they taste?

I didn't want to wait until Trevor and Maya got there to see if they were any good. If they were terrible, I needed to be the first to know. I picked up a whoopie pie and took a bite.

It. Was. Delicious. It tasted kind of like a red velvet cupcake, but easier to eat since the frosting was in the middle. The pecans added a nice crunch and flavor that brought the whoopie pie to another level. I finished the entire thing and stopped myself from eating another one.

After I cleaned up and ate dinner, Trevor and Maya came over. It was the first time just the three of us were hanging out since our movie night, when I first realized they liked each other. I was a little nervous about feeling like the third wheel again, but I pushed those thoughts aside. They were here for me—for my whoopie pies too, but mostly for me.

"Wow," Maya said when she saw the platter of whoopie pies. "They're so pretty."

"Yeah," Trevor said. "Your chocolate ones looked nice too, but these look like they're from a cookbook cover or something."

"Thanks!" I smiled. "Try one."

I watched as they each grabbed a whoopie pie and took a bite. Even though I knew they tasted good, my heart started beating a little faster. But then I saw Maya grin and nod after every bite. Trevor practically inhaled his.

"Okay, be honest," I said. "Would you change anything?

Does it need more of something?"

"It's perfect, Zo," Maya said. "Like, straight out of a bakery, perfect."

"Really?"

"If I gave your other whoopie pies a hundred out of ten, I give these a thousand," Trevor said. "Those little nuts or whatever inside? Incredible."

I beamed with pride, and any remaining stress from the day melted away. "I'm so happy you like them."

Now I needed to make sure Marcus liked them and was okay with us selling them on our food truck. I decided to make them again for our next Sunday dinner, which would be the day after our event.

Maya, Trevor, and I hung out for a while longer, talking and watching funny videos on Trevor's phone.

When Maya's mom arrived to pick her up, we went to the front door and Maya said she wanted to talk to me alone for a second. We said bye to Trevor, and Maya waved at her mom in the car.

"I've been dying to tell you something," she said in a low voice. "Trevor and I . . . we finally kissed."

My mouth fell open. "You did? Ahh, how was it? I mean, don't get too detailed. Trevor's still like my brother. But . . . was it nice?"

Maya's face lit up. "So nice. Kind of awkward for the

first few seconds, but it got way better after that. I mean, he's the sweetest guy. He asked me if he could kiss me before he did it."

"Of course he did. Trevor is a good guy. I can't believe he was your first kiss!"

Maya blushed, and we hugged.

On Wednesday, three days before the event, Marcus and I still hadn't confirmed our panelists.

Marcus suggested we check out another landmark on the Black Heritage Trail during our lunch break so I could clear my mind and think about something else. I knew nothing would get my mind off the event, but I agreed to go anyway.

We walked to the Charles Street Meeting House, which Marcus told me was once home to the first integrated church in America. The building looked like a church, with its tall windows and arched doorways. It also had a big clock at the top.

"Apparently the First African Methodist Episcopal congregation went on to buy this building in the 1870s," Marcus said, reading from the trail website on his phone. "They eventually moved to a different location in the 1930s, but in between then, local activists would meet here too. Interesting, right?"

All I could do was nod. It *was* interesting, but my thoughts were somewhere else. The pit in my stomach was growing and I couldn't take it anymore.

"Can we talk about Saturday instead?" I asked Marcus. "We still don't have any panelists." So far, Claire hadn't been able to find anyone else at the Innocence Project who was available. "I could just interview you, and we could talk about our story again. But then it wouldn't be a panel and—"

Marcus cut me off. "Little T."

I exhaled. "Yes?"

"We still have a potential panelist," he said. "Christina Stone, the one who works for Fresh Start. I know you said you wanted to wait to see if anyone else was free. But I talked to Christina again yesterday, and she's still interested—and available. She also said she has a colleague who went to prison for his crimes but is out now. His name is Daniel, and he acts as a mentor to people newly freed from prison. Christina said she could ask him to be on the panel too."

"But then it wouldn't be a panel about exonerees," I said. "That's the whole point of my podcast right now."

"True," Marcus said. "But if you're willing to broaden the topic, we could make the event about what life is like after prison for all kinds of people—those who were wrongfully convicted, and those who committed their crimes. I can still be on the panel to share my perspective as an exoneree."

I thought about Marcus's proposal—having him, Christina, and Daniel on the panel. It'd mean having a slightly different panel discussion than I'd originally planned, but at least we'd have *something*. And after talking to Hannah, I did wonder what Christina had to say. Maybe other people in the audience would be interested, too.

"One other thing," Marcus said. "Christina said she'd email their company mailing list about the event, whether she's on the panel or not, since she thinks their community will be interested in checking it out. And she'll be there on Saturday too, either way. She thinks it's fantastic that at your age, you're doing something like this."

Wow. Christina was being so supportive, and she hadn't even met me.

"Okay," I finally said.

"Okay, as in yes to Christina and Daniel?"

"And you, too. Yes to all three of you as panelists."

Marcus smiled. "I think this is going to be great. And you're going to learn so much from what Christina and Daniel have to say."

I nodded. Already I could think of some questions for them. Like, what kind of things did Daniel do as a mentor? And what made Christina want to work at Fresh Start? I wanted to meet them and learn more.

I'd been telling myself lately that I needed to be more open-minded.

Now was my chance to do it.

Chapter Thirty-Six

On the day of our event, I woke up with a massive stomachache.

I'd been so focused on planning over the last nine days that it hadn't sunk in yet that I was about to stand onstage in front of who knew how many people. Was I really about to host a live podcast? I didn't know anything about public speaking, and I'd never hosted an event before. What if I messed up? What if I forgot what to say? What if I threw up onstage?

All these thoughts appeared before I even got out of bed.

Then I opened my window blinds.

Oh no.

It was raining. And not just a little rain, but an actual shower.

My stomachache grew. It was supposed to be partly sunny today! I hadn't checked the weather app in a few days because I'd been so busy with everything else. I checked it again now and saw that the forecast had changed to partly cloudy, with scattered showers.

No no no.

I clicked on the hourly forecast to see what time it was going to rain. The app said now, and then again at two p.m. Then it looked like the rest of the afternoon would be cloudy.

These apps weren't always accurate. What if it rained later than two p.m.? What if it didn't stop raining before our event started at four?

Would anybody show up to our event in the rain? The bandshell and the area around it was all open. Maybe people would still come with umbrellas. But what were the odds of that?

Why would someone come to a last-minute event hosted by a random kid even if it *wasn't* raining?

I sank back onto my bed, suddenly feeling like I'd made a huge mistake.

There was a knock on my door.

"Come in," I mumbled.

Mom opened the door and saw me hugging my pillow.

"As soon as I saw the rain, I knew you'd be upset," she said, joining me on my bed. "But it looks like it's going to clear up, so don't worry."

"What if it doesn't?" I asked.

I grabbed my phone and called Marcus, putting it on speaker.

"Have you looked outside?" I asked as soon as he answered.

"I have," Marcus said. "But I'm not worried about any rain. This show's going on, no matter what."

"Even if nobody shows up?"

"We'll make it work," Marcus said. "Don't stress."

"We can't control the weather, and we can't control whether anyone shows up," Mom said. "But you know what we can control? We can make sure we finish everything on our to-do list and give it our best effort today. So, c'mon. Get dressed and let's eat some breakfast so you have energy for the day. We'll take it one step at a time."

"What your mom said," Marcus chimed in.

"Okay." I told Marcus I'd see him later and got up to get dressed.

What other choice did I have?

* * *

At three o'clock, my parents, Grandma, Marcus, and I arrived at the bandshell. We'd planned to get there early to set up. Christina and Daniel were also going to meet us so we could go over the event schedule.

It'd stopped raining earlier in the afternoon but started up again around two thirty. It was still raining, but only lightly, when we got to the bandshell. We all brought umbrellas and rain jackets.

"What if people think it's canceled?" I asked out loud to nobody in particular once we parked in the lot.

"Do you have any control over that?" Mom asked me.

"No . . ."

"Then don't think about that. Just focus on setting up."

"The rain is supposed to stop at three thirty," Dad said, reassuringly.

I held on to hope that it would as we all got to work.

Dad carried the speaker that we'd rented up onto the stage. He'd offered to cover the cost to rent a speaker and a couple of microphones for me and the panelists to share. We also brought four folding chairs for the stage.

Marcus helped my mom carry a folding table that we had in our basement. We were going to use it for the cupcake and lemonade samples Ariana was providing. She was going to bring a tablecloth and some other decorations to make it look pretty.

My parents also brought some of our beach chairs and a blanket, so they could sit in the audience with Grandma to watch the panel.

"There's Christina and Daniel," Marcus said once we finished arranging the chairs and equipment on the stage. "Right on time."

Marcus and I got down from the bandshell to meet them. Christina held an umbrella and Daniel had on a windbreaker and baseball hat.

Don't think about the rain, I reminded myself. *Focus on what you can control.*

Christina smiled as she approached us. "Some people say rain before an event is good luck, so this bodes well."

I liked her already. She was almost as tall as Marcus and had a commanding presence. But she seemed warm, not intimidating.

Daniel was a larger man with a kind face. But behind his eyes, you could tell he'd been through some hard times. I couldn't help but wonder what he'd gone to prison for.

"Thanks for inviting us to be part of this," Daniel said after we all did introductions.

Christina nodded. "This is going to be great. Zoe, what's the game plan?"

"Oh, um," I said, and I opened the app on my phone where I had my notes and questions. "Right, so, uh . . ."

"Hold on there a second," Christina said, and I looked up at her. "I need you to start over, with more confidence this time. I've listened to your podcast, so I know you've got it in you."

Did I? I couldn't seem to shake my nerves.

Christina gave me a warm smile. "I've had to talk in front of a lot of people, and I know how nerve-racking it can be. But you've got this, sweetheart. When we get on that stage, pretend it's us up there recording another episode of your podcast.

"Also, sometimes it's helpful to think of your 'why.' Why did you want to put this panel together? Who is this for? You can even pick one person in the audience to focus on."

I thought about why I had put this panel together— to spread awareness about life after incarceration, and to help our Kickstarter succeed. Both of those mattered way more than the butterflies in my stomach.

"Thanks for the advice," I said, my voice more confident. "Okay, here's the plan . . ."

I went over the program order and the questions I planned to ask them and Marcus. Not long after that, Ariana arrived to set up her snacks.

And then the most amazing thing happened. The rain stopped and the sun appeared behind the clouds! My parents had a few beach towels in the car, so we used them to wipe down everything onstage, plus the folding table.

The rain had stopped just in time, but would people still come? Would they think it was still too wet?

At a quarter to four, all that was left to do was wait to see who showed up.

The first people I spotted were my friends. Trevor came with his parents, Maya came with her mom and sister, and Hannah came with her dad and brother.

"Thank you so much for coming!" I told all of them.

"Break a leg!" Maya said.

"What?" Trevor said to her. "Why would you say that?"

"It's an expression people say in the theater," Maya said, giggling. "How have you not heard of that?"

Then Hannah said, "I wouldn't have missed this for anything. Ever since I've been writing to my mom, I've been thinking about this topic a lot. I'm really glad you're doing this."

My heart swelled. Even if nobody else showed up, I was happy that this panel conversation might help Hannah. She could be the person I focused on if I got nervous. She was another one of my "whys."

It was nice to finally be able to introduce her to Trevor and Maya. I gave them the flyers we'd printed with the Kickstarter information and QR code. They'd agreed to hand them out to the audience as they arrived.

Then I noticed cars starting to pull into the lot next to the bandshell. More than a few cars. As people got out, some were holding camping chairs or large outdoor blankets. There were both kids and adults. People of all ethnicities. Some went right over to Ariana's table to grab a cupcake and cup of lemonade, and others set up their chairs in front of the stage first.

People were showing up to our event!

As they settled into their seats, I started doing mental calculations. If everyone here contributed to our Kickstarter, could it be enough to get us to the finish line?

I had no idea. But I couldn't spend any more time thinking about it.

I had a panel to host, and it was showtime.

Chapter Thirty-Seven

I cleared my throat and turned on my microphone. "Hi, everybody." The mic screeched, which made me jump. On the side of the bandshell, Dad adjusted the speaker controls and then gave me a thumbs-up to keep going.

"Testing . . ." This time the mic volume was much better. "Sorry about that. Um . . ."

I remembered what Christina had said about being confident. Even though my hands were shaking, I made my voice strong and clear. "Thank you all for coming today. I'm Zoe Washington, and I'm a baker, a soon-to-be ninth grader, and the host of the podcast *On Air with Zoe*

Washington. Maybe you've gotten the chance to listen to it before coming here today." I quickly described what the podcast was all about and shared how to subscribe.

"I started this podcast and we're having this event today because I want things to change. I want . . ."—I started to say "exonerees" but then remembered that wasn't the sole focus of our event anymore—". . . *people* who've been incarcerated to be able to get back to their lives, without having to struggle to meet their basic needs. They deserve that."

I locked eyes with Hannah in the audience. She grinned at me, and I took a second to remember my whys before introducing Marcus, Christina, and Daniel.

"Let's dive into our questions," I said. "First, Christina, can you tell me about your role at the organization you work for?"

"Absolutely," Christina said. "I'm a case manager at Fresh Start, and what I do is help previously incarcerated individuals get re-entry services, so they can get back on their feet after prison. I start talking to inmates before they are even released, to help them get started with these services. The two biggest struggles they experience are finding housing and employment, so we help them in those areas the most."

Christina was a natural public speaker. She spoke into

her mic slowly and passionately.

"What do you wish everyone knew about the people you work with?" I asked.

"That often, their crimes were a result of a lack of education and family support growing up. For example, many of the men I work with never finished high school. That also makes it hard when they're out of prison. Then, not only do they have difficulty getting a job because of their record, they also don't have the education needed to qualify for certain jobs."

I thought about how Marcus had been able to get a college degree while locked up. "Could they finish high school while they're in prison?" I asked.

Christina nodded. "There are programs that help inmates get their GED, yes. But not everyone is able to make that happen.

"Also, a lot of these men never had a father or a father figure in their life," Christina continued. "So, they didn't have someone to show them the proper way to do things, or to teach them right and wrong. Some grew up with grandparents because their own parents were incarcerated. And some had literally never left the couple-mile radius of their neighborhoods, which are often high crime areas where they saw nothing but violence their whole lives. Some are still dealing with untreated trauma from their childhoods. I could go on, but you get the gist."

"Wow," I said. "I honestly never thought about what they might have gone through before they went to prison." Of course, it made sense that if a kid had a tough childhood, and didn't have positive role models in their life, that they might end up doing something illegal.

Christina nodded. "You're not the only one. People make assumptions about folks who've come out of prison without knowing anything about their backgrounds or childhoods."

"So, you think if they'd had better childhoods, a lot of the people you work with wouldn't have committed any crimes?" I asked.

"In a lot of cases, yes," Christina said. "So many factors lead to crime. Sometimes people are drawn to it because they truly don't know any better. Sometimes they commit crimes to survive. Our job at Fresh Start is to help these folks, to show them that there are alternatives. That's why it's especially important to have Daniel on our team, since he's been through something similar."

Christina turned to Daniel, so I glanced his way too. The nerves I'd felt about interviewing someone who'd committed a crime lingered. But I reminded myself that he worked at Fresh Start to help others, to make a difference. I wanted to know how. So, after a breath, I asked him, "What do you do at Fresh Start?"

Daniel took the microphone from Christina. "I'm a community advocate."

Already I could tell he was more soft-spoken than Christina.

He went on, his voice calm and intentional. "I help Christina with everything she mentioned, but I also act as a mentor." He paused. "I want to show people that there *is* life beyond what they knew before they went to prison."

I nodded.

"I've been in their shoes, you know?" Daniel said. "I know how dark your mind can get while in a cell. How easy it is to keep being the same troubled person who got locked up in the first place." He paused again. "But I also know it's possible to change. And just because you're in prison, it's never too late to start changing once you're there."

"How can they do that?" I asked.

"They can start working on themselves before they get out."

I was about to ask for an example when Daniel said, "They can take advantage of the programs available to prisoners, like getting their GED. They can work on whatever personal issues they may have, and distance themselves from other inmates who have a negative impact on them."

"Do you see a lot of people making those positive changes?" I asked.

"Yes," Daniel said. "They just need the encouragement and support. I know exactly what they're going through, so I try to be there for them."

"That's so great," I said, and I meant it. Daniel seemed so sincere.

I shifted in my seat, suddenly revved up about how well this panel was going so far.

"My next question is for Marcus," I said, peering at my notes. "As someone who was in prison for a crime that you didn't commit, what do you think about the people who were guilty of their crimes?"

"I don't have any bias toward them," Marcus said after taking the mic from Daniel. "I'm in awe of people like Daniel who are able to turn their lives around and do better. I may not have that exact experience, but I know what it's like to get out of prison and feel the weight of having to start over. I want to help people, too. Like, by offering employment, if we're able to get our food truck off the ground."

"That's amazing," Christina said to Marcus. "It would

make such a big difference if more employers were willing to do that."

I'd been against Marcus's plan to hire previously incarcerated people from the start. And then I had been hesitant to add Christina and Daniel to this panel. But why? Why was I so scared of helping people who'd committed a crime? I found Hannah in the audience again, and thought of her mom, who I hoped would get the kind of support Fresh Start offered. And I looked at Daniel, who had gone to prison after committing a crime, and was now helping people, inspiring them to do better.

I needed to do better. I needed to stop judging and remember that previous offenders were like many of us—worthy of another chance. Like Hannah, I wanted to believe they could change and do better. If I wanted things to be better for Marcus, I had to try to make them better for others, too.

I decided right then that if our food truck got funded and we were able to open it, I'd agree to hire someone out of prison, to give them a chance to start over.

"I hope we're able to help someone like that," I said to Marcus.

Marcus smiled, and I could tell he was surprised to hear me say that.

"Speaking of the food truck," I said, "I want to quickly

tell you all about our Kickstarter." I briefly explained Marcus's and my plan to open our Big and Little BBQ Truck. "Donating is totally optional, but we'd really appreciate your help."

Once that was out of the way, I turned back to our panelists. "Marcus, can you talk about what struggles you've experienced since getting out of prison? Even though you were wrongfully convicted?"

"Of course." Marcus went on to tell his story of going to prison, being exonerated, and how he hadn't been able to get exoneree compensation from the state, or any other assistance or loans.

I asked Marcus, Christina, and Daniel a few more questions, and then we opened it up for audience Q&A. There were even some other prior inmates in the crowd, and they shared some of their stories as well.

I learned so much from all of them, and in the end, I was happy the panel topic had shifted to include prior inmates who had committed their crimes. Because they deserved grace, support, and a better life, too.

Chapter Thirty-Eight

My body was so pumped full of adrenaline by the time our event ended that I could barely process the applause. People—strangers, even—were clapping for us! Mom, Dad, Grandma, and my friends cheered the loudest, of course. The grassy area in front of the bandshell hadn't totally filled up, but we'd gotten a good crowd in the end. There were people who'd heard about our event through Christina, some who'd come after getting our flyer at the farmers market, and some who'd seen the event on the bandshell website. Not only did they all watch the panel, but many stayed around for a while after it, eating Ariana's cupcakes, continuing the conversation, and connecting with one another.

All because I'd had this event.

I'd done it!

After we cleaned and packed up, got home, and ate dinner, I totally crashed on the couch. I didn't check Kickstarter to see if anyone who'd attended the event donated. For now, I wanted to focus on how proud I felt. I'd gotten the community talking about life after incarceration.

I'd really done it.

Sunday was the day before our Kickstarter deadline. We had until 11:59 p.m. on Monday night to meet our goal. Marcus and I decided to wait until dinner that night to check the numbers. It felt right to wait until our family was all together. If it was good news, we could celebrate. If it was bad news, we could be there for each other.

I asked him and Grandma if I could invite Trevor, Maya, and Hannah for dinner. They were both fine with it. I was excited to hang out with my three best friends, together.

Since we were going to be a larger group, Marcus decided to make a big batch of pulled pork and serve it as sandwiches. He also made seasoned potato wedges and a sweet corn salad.

For dessert, I made a larger batch of the red velvet

whoopie pies. I was excited for everyone to try them, and to celebrate in general. No matter what happened with the Kickstarter, I wanted to celebrate all our hard work—what we'd done in the past month to get the Kickstarter together, and especially the event we'd pulled off yesterday.

Marcus and I were in great moods while we cooked and baked. We jammed out to the Little Tomato playlist the entire time.

When my parents and friends arrived later, it felt like we were having a holiday dinner, not just another Sunday one. It felt more special somehow.

"You know this is our eighth Sunday dinner?" I said to Marcus as I helped him put the food on platters to bring to the dining room.

"For real?" he said.

"Yeah. I counted them this morning."

"Wow. That's great."

"I'm so glad you suggested that we do this," I said. "And that we've had this time together. And that you're finally out of prison."

"Do you want to make me cry over this sweet corn?" Marcus asked with a laugh. Then he said, "Little T, even with the challenges I've been dealing with after prison,

I am still having the best time of my life. I am truly blessed."

I smiled.

"Let's bring this food out there before it gets cold," he said.

In the dining room, we held hands around the table so Marcus could bless the food. Then we all dug in. Everything was delicious as usual, so for a few minutes we all ate and savored it quietly.

Then Trevor asked, "So, Zoe, how much longer are you going to wait to check the Kickstarter?"

"Oh yeah," Maya said. "I know you told us not to check it before tonight, but you must be dying to know."

"It's not even my food truck, and I'm dying to know," Hannah said.

"Let's get through dinner first," I said, thinking about our original plan. "We can check right before dessert."

After a beat, Marcus said, ". . . or we can check it now."

"You want to?" I asked.

"Let's just do it," he said. "We already know we're happy no matter what happens."

"Yes! Let's see those numbers," Grandma said.

"Okay," I said. "Let me pull it up on my phone." My heart started racing.

"We should do a drumroll," Trevor said. He started lightly drumming the table, and everyone joined in.

Hands shaking, I opened the Kickstarter page and looked at the total.

The room got silent.

My heart sank when I saw the number: $18,900. We were at 63 percent of our goal. We'd gotten more donations after our event, but it wasn't enough.

It wasn't enough.

And with only a little over twenty-four hours until the deadline, it probably would never be enough.

My eyes welled up with tears. Mom came over and put her arms around me as she peered at my phone screen.

The room stayed silent as everyone understood.

"I'm sorry, kiddo," Dad said.

I tried to blink the tears back, but it didn't work. I buried my face in my hands and cried. I couldn't bear to look at Marcus and see the disappointment on his face.

I'd let him down. This was all my fault. We never should've started the Kickstarter. I never should've believed that this could work.

Suddenly, I felt someone else's hand squeeze my shoulder. "It's okay," Marcus whispered in my ear. "It's going to be okay. There's still time, you know. More people from yesterday might donate."

It wasn't okay, but I didn't say anything.

I stood up, and without looking at anyone, walked down the hall and into the bathroom, closing the door behind me.

"I know what'll cheer everybody up," I heard Trevor say from the dining room. "You've gotta try Zoe's red velvet whoopie pies. They're one of the best things I've ever tasted."

"*Trev*," I heard Maya say. "Seriously?"

"What? I think they'll really cheer everyone up!"

I knew I'd said I wanted to celebrate no matter what. But that was a lie. I couldn't stand to look at the whoopie pies, which would only remind me that I wouldn't get to serve them on our food truck. All I wanted to do was go home and crawl into bed.

Chapter Thirty-Nine

On Monday, I slogged my way through getting ready for work. Marcus and Grandma picked me up as usual.

"How're you feeling today, baby?" Grandma asked when I got into the back seat of her car. "You look tired."

"I didn't sleep well," I said.

Marcus turned around to face me. "I hate seeing you so upset."

"I know. I just feel like I let you down."

"You could never let me down, Little T," Marcus said, his voice serious. "The donations were always out of our control, and you did everything you could. We'll find another way to open our food truck. I know it."

That was what Trevor, Maya, and Hannah had said, too. Trevor and Maya had sent me encouraging messages on our group chat, and Hannah also texted cute dog videos to cheer me up.

I nodded and leaned against the car window, closing my eyes for the rest of the ride.

Work was busy, which was good because I didn't have the chance to feel tired.

During our lunch break, Marcus asked if I wanted to get pizza and check out another Black Heritage Trail stop. "My treat," he said.

"Sure."

"Okay, I'll meet you outside."

I stood outside the shop, watching a video Hannah had sent of an adult golden retriever meeting the family's new puppy for the first time. I almost cried from the cuteness. Two minutes later, Marcus burst through the Ari's Cakes entrance.

"Little T, look at this," he said, shoving his phone at me.

"What?"

I glanced at his phone screen, which was opened to our Kickstarter. I was about to push it away, since I didn't want to know, but then I saw it.

"Oh my god," I said.

The little green bar at the top that showed our progress was completely filled in. We'd done it. Our Kickstarter was fully funded! Somehow, we'd exceeded our goal, with 127 percent of it funded.

"*What? How?*" My hands shook as I took the phone from Marcus.

I noticed the number of backer comments had gone up, so I clicked over and scrolled through them.

"Saw the BPR post and heard your interview. You're an inspiration! Can't wait to come visit your food truck and meet you in person!"

"Came here after listening to your Boston Public Radio interview. Wow, what a story. Good luck!"

"Hope this helps. Loved your interview!"

Wait. What?

I went to the Boston Public Radio website and clicked on their social media pages. I scrolled until I found it.

Even though Tyler at the radio station never replied to my last email, he'd shared my Kickstarter link, along with our interview, on Boston Public Radio's social media the night before. He hadn't tagged me, and I hadn't thought to check their social media. I'd had no idea. The posts had a ton of likes, shares, and comments.

"This is amazing," I said. "Boston Public Radio posted

about the Kickstarter and a bunch of random people on the internet contributed!"

"Really?" Marcus asked.

"Yes. Oh my gosh." I was still in shock.

"But how?" Marcus asked. "How did they find out about the Kickstarter?"

"I reached out to them before our event and sent them the link."

"Wow," Marcus said. "You really thought of everything."

"I never heard back, so I thought they'd ignored my email," I said. "But I guess not!"

"You made this happen, Zoe," Marcus said. "I'm so proud."

"I'm proud of both of us," I said.

It was like we'd come full circle. Marcus had first told me about his restaurant dream during our lunch break outside Ari's Cakes. And now we'd just found out our food truck dream was coming true in basically the same spot.

Maybe Marcus had the same thought, because when I looked up at him, he was tearing up. As soon as he wrapped his arms around me, I lost it. But they were some of the happiest tears I'd ever cried.

Eight Months Later

"What do you think?" I asked Marcus, who was at the back of the truck, finishing up prepping food. "Are we ready to open? There's already a line outside."

"I think we're good to go," he said. "All the food's prepped for orders. How are you feeling about your desserts?"

"Great," I said. "The red velvet whoopie pies look and taste amazing."

"Lisa, you ready to take orders?" Marcus asked.

Marcus had hired Lisa, who he met through Fresh Start, a month earlier. She had gotten out of prison not long ago and had been looking for a job. She was a mom

288

and eager to get her life back in order for her son. But that was only part of her story. She was also funny and personable and had waitressing experience from before prison. Both Marcus and I were excited to have her join the Big and Little BBQ family.

"Sure am, boss," Lisa said.

"All right, then," Marcus said. "Let's open up."

As soon as Marcus, Lisa, and I walked off the truck in our matching red Big and Little BBQ aprons, there was a round of applause. Mom was right in front, taking pictures of us with her phone, and Dad stood next to her holding a bouquet of flowers. Beside them, Grandma had the biggest grin and tears of pride in her eyes. Maya and Trevor were there too, holding hands. With her free hand, Maya waved one of her cheerleading pom-poms in the air. I also spotted Hannah with her dad and brother. Ariana had come with her husband. Even some of Trevor's basketball teammates showed up. I grinned at everybody.

It wasn't only familiar faces either. There were also Kickstarter funders who'd come to celebrate our grand opening.

After months of preparation, using the Kickstarter funds to rent a truck, get it wrapped in vinyl with our branding, plus pay for permits, licenses, and supplies, we were finally ready to start serving customers. We'd decided to park in the bandshell parking lot on farmers market day, when lots of people would be around. We arrived right before lunchtime.

"Thanks, everyone, for being here," Marcus said to the crowd. "I'll keep this short and sweet since I know you're all ready to try some barbecue and whoopie pies." He winked at me and put his arm around my shoulder. "Zoe and I are so grateful for your support. We couldn't have done any of this without you. Thank you so much for being here today." He looked at me. "Little T, do you want to say anything?"

My cheeks got hot. Even after hosting that live podcast event months earlier, I still didn't love public speaking. But I took a deep breath and said, "Just that I hope you enjoy our food! And please tell all your friends about us. Also, we should introduce you to Lisa, the newest member of our team. She'll help take your orders."

Lisa gave a small wave and smiled. "Hey, y'all! I'm so happy to be here with Marcus and Zoe. Let me know what we can get you."

We'd come up with a system for orders. I would stay in the truck helping Marcus serve. Once Lisa took an order, she'd put it on a ticket and hand that to me. I'd hang the ticket near the prep area so Marcus could prepare the order, and then when it was ready, I'd pass it to Lisa to give out. If someone ordered dessert, I'd handle that.

We spent the next couple hours serving orders like this and talking to customers who'd come just to see us.

A local news reporter even came by! He said his station was going to run a story the next day about our journey to opening the truck.

When the customer orders finally died down, Marcus and I got off the truck for some fresh air.

"Zoe!"

I turned toward my name to find Hannah. "Oh hey!" I walked up to her.

"You were so busy before, but I didn't want to leave without saying hi," she said. "The truck looks amazing, and the food tasted incredible. The whoopie pies were even better than I remembered."

"I'm so glad you liked everything!" I said. "How are things with you?" Since we went to schools in different towns, we hadn't seen each other much lately.

"Good. Did I tell you I'm visiting my mom next weekend?"

"No! Really?"

"Yeah. Things are getting better between us, after writing letters and then having some phone calls," Hannah said. "I decided I'm finally ready to see her in person again."

"I'm so happy for you," I said. "I hope it goes well. Make sure you bring change for the vending machines."

She smiled. "I will. Anyway, I have to go now. My dad's waiting for me. But congrats again! You're officially the coolest person I know."

"No, you are," I said, and we hugged.

When I got back to the truck, Marcus was closing the concession window. I loved the satisfying click it made every time it locked into place.

"Before I go, here are the cards," Lisa said, handing Marcus a small box.

We'd asked her to give out comment cards with each order so we could get feedback on the food and service from everybody.

"Thanks, Lisa," Marcus said. "For everything today. Get home safe."

Lisa headed to her car, and I grabbed a couple of comment cards from the box to read. "This one says, 'My pulled pork sandwich was excellent.' Oh, and they loved the whoopie pies, too!" I beamed and read another one. "This person said they can't wait to come back every weekend so they can taste our entire menu. I bet we'll start having regulars!"

Marcus took one of the cards. "This says, 'My meal didn't disappoint. Telling my friends!'" He looked at me.

"I'd say day one was a success."

I grinned.

"Ready to head out?" he asked.

"Yup."

Before Marcus walked over to the driver's side, he took in the truck, which was covered in red vinyl and had "Big and Little BBQ" on each side in huge white letters. His face was full of pride.

I was proud too—of Marcus for making it through all his hardships after prison, and of the two of us for making this dream happen.

Standing next to him, I rested my head against his arm. I couldn't wait to see what we did next.

Acknowledgments

When From the Desk of Zoe Washington was first published, I never planned to write a sequel. I thought it'd be a stand-alone novel since the story wraps up in the epilogue. But once I started doing school visits, the most common question students asked was, "Is there going to be a sequel?" For the longest time, my answer was no. But as I kept getting that question, I started to wonder if I *should* continue Zoe's and Marcus's stories. Then I realized that there were more questions I could answer in a second book. Like, what is Marcus's life like after prison? How does his relationship with Zoe grow and change? What is next for Zoe's baking? Is she still best friends with Trevor?

I hope that by reading On Air with Zoe Washington, you enjoy discovering the answers to these questions and returning to the world of these beloved characters. So, thank you to all the young readers who encouraged and inspired me to make this book happen!

I also want to thank my editor, Mabel Hsu, for all her advice and expertise as I developed and revised this story. You're a dream to work with!

To Katherine Tegen, Julia Johnson, Vaishali Nayak, Aubrey Churchward, Laura Harshberger, Jennifer Sale, Mark Rifkin, Erin Wallace, Kristen Eckhardt, Laura Mock, Amy Ryan, Ann Dye, Patty Rosati, Mimi Rankin, and Katie Dutton: Thank you for helping my Zoe Washington books find their audience. I couldn't be prouder to be a HarperCollins Katherine Tegen Book author!

Thank you to Mirelle Ortega for illustrating another gorgeous cover, as well as the adorable chapter openers inside!

I also want to thank Mary Loftus and William Outlaw for sharing their knowledge on life after incarceration. It was very important for me to represent this topic authentically, so I appreciate you taking the time to educate me.

As always, thank you to my agent, Alex Slater, for helping me get my books out there, and for guiding me through this journey. Thanks as well to the Trident Media

Group team for all your support.

To my husband, daughter, family, and friends: Thank you for your love and enthusiasm whenever I have publishing news to share.

As I write this, books like mine are being banned and challenged at schools and in libraries around the country. I want to thank all the librarians, educators, booksellers, and bloggers who have continued to support and share my books despite this. You're the best.

Finally, thank you to everyone who's read and shared my books. Publishing *From the Desk of Zoe Washington* changed my life, and because of you, I now have my dream job. I am forever grateful.